KU-477-571

Scarlet Wilson wrote her first story aged eight and has never stopped. She's worked in the health service for twenty years, having trained as a nurse and a health visitor. Scarlet now works in public health and lives on the West Coast of Scotland with her fiancé and their two sons. Writing medical romances and contemporary romances is a dream come true for her.

Also by Scarlet Wilson

Locked Down with the Army Doc
Cinderella's New York Christmas
Island Doctor to Royal Bride?
Tempted by the Hot Highland Doc

The Good Luck Hospital miniseries

Healing the Single Dad's Heart
Just Friends to Just Married?

Discover more at millsandboon.co.uk.

JUST FRIENDS TO JUST MARRIED?

SCARLET WILSON

MILLS & BOON

All rights reserved including the right of reproduction
in whole or in part in any form. This edition is published
by arrangement with Harlequin Books S.A.

This is a work of fiction. Names, characters, places, locations
and incidents are purely fictional and bear no relationship to
any real life individuals, living or dead, or to any actual places,
business establishments, locations, events or incidents.
Any resemblance is entirely coincidental.

This book is sold subject to the condition that it shall not,
by way of trade or otherwise, be lent, resold, hired out
or otherwise circulated without the prior consent of the publisher
in any form of binding or cover other than that in which it is published
and without a similar condition including this condition
being imposed on the subsequent purchaser.

® and TM are trademarks owned and used by the trademark owner
and/or its licensee. Trademarks marked with ® are registered with the
United Kingdom Patent Office and/or the Office for Harmonisation
in the Internal Market and in other countries.

Published in Great Britain 2019
by Mills & Boon, an imprint of HarperCollins*Publishers*
1 London Bridge Street, London, SE1 9GF

© 2019 Scarlet Wilson

ISBN: 978-0-263-08073-5

MIX
Paper from
responsible sources
FSC® **C007454**

This book is produced from independently certified FSC™ paper
to ensure responsible forest management.
For more information visit www.harpercollins.co.uk/green.

Printed and bound in Great Britain
by CPI Group (UK) Ltd, Croydon, CR0 4YY

This book is dedicated to all my best boys:
Noah Dickson, Lleyton Hyndman and Luca Dickson.
Love you guys!

CHAPTER ONE

THE SHRILL OF the phone cut through the dark night.

Vivienne Kerr fought her way free of the tangled sheets, her brain desperately trying to make sense of the noise. Was she on call? Was this a home delivery?

By the time she reached for the phone she was shaking her head. No. Definitely not on call. Not tonight. She'd been on call for the last three nights in a row. This was her first night off.

Or maybe it was morning. Maybe she'd slept for more than twenty-four hours and was late for her next shift…

Her eyes glanced at the green lights of her clock. Three thirty-seven. Her heart sank. Nope. She definitely wasn't late, and no normal person would phone at this time of night—not unless it was bad news.

She picked up the phone, sucking in a breath as if, in some way, it would protect her from what would come next.

She was practically praying that this would be a wrong number. Someone looking for a taxi, or someone with crazy middle-of-the-night hunger pangs that could only be filled with some kind of takeaway food, or even a drunken call from some guy she'd previously given her number to. She'd take any of the above.

'Hello?'

For a few seconds there wasn't really a reply.

Every tiny hair on her bare arms stood on end. She swung her legs from the bed and sat bolt upright. All her instincts were on edge. Her stomach clenched.

'Hello?' she tried again.

There was a noise at the end of the phone. She couldn't quite work out if it was a sob or a choke. 'Viv.'

The voice stopped, as if it had taken all their effort just to say her name. She'd recognise that voice anywhere.

'Duc?' Panic gripped her. Her best friend. Where was he working now—Washington? Philadelphia? She moved into work mode. The way she acted when everything that could go wrong at a delivery did go wrong.

Take charge.

'Duc? What's wrong? Where are you? Are you okay?'

Every tiny fragment of patience that she'd ever had had just flown out of the window. Duc. As she squeezed her eyes shut, she could see his floppy brown hair and soft brown eyes in her head. Duc. They'd met at a teaching hospital in London while she'd been a midwifery student and he'd been a medical student. No one could have predicted how much the crazy, rootless Scottish girl would click with the ever cheerful, laughing Vietnamese boy.

It was fate. It was…kind of magic.

A clinical emergency had floored them both. A young mother with an undiagnosed placenta praevia. Both had only been in the room to observe. Both had had no experience of a situation like this before. The mother had haemorrhaged rapidly, leading to the delivery of a very blue baby. Both Vivienne and Duc had ended up at either side of the bed, squeezing in emergency units of blood at almost the same rate as it appeared to be coming back out of the poor mother. It seemed that every rule in the book had gone out of the window in the attempt to save both baby and mum.

By the time things had come to a conclusion with mum rushed to emergency surgery, and baby rushed to the NICU, Duc and Vivienne had been left in the remnants of the room, with almost every surface, them included, splattered with blood.

Vivienne had done her best to hold it together. And she'd managed it. Almost.

Right until she'd reached the sluice room to dispose of aprons and gloves. Then she'd started to shake and cry. When the slim but strong arms had slid around her waist without a word, and Duc had rested his head on her shoulder, she'd realised that he had been shaking too. He'd known not to try and speak to her. He'd known not to ask her if she wanted a hug. He'd just acted, and they'd stood there, undisturbed, for nearly five minutes, cementing their friendship for ever.

But now? Fear gripped her chest. Duc hadn't answered.

Worst-case scenarios started shooting through her brain. He was sick. He was injured. Something terrible had happened to him.

'Duc? Talk to me, please. I need to know how you are. I need to know that you're okay.'

'I…I…I need you.'

She was on her feet in an instant, looking frantically around her room. She clenched the phone between the crook of her neck and her ear as she fell to her knees and pulled a bag from the bottom of her cupboard.

'I'll be there.' She'd never been surer of anything in her life. 'Where are you? What's wrong?'

'It's...*mẹ va cha*.'

She recognised the Vietnamese words instantly. 'Your mum and dad? Duc, what's happened? Are they hurt?'

Her stomach clenched. She'd met Khiem and Hoa on a few occasions. They were a charming couple, completely devoted to the hospitals they ran in Hanoi and two other outlying areas in Vietnam.

Silence filled her ears and an ache spread across her chest. Experience told her that silence usually meant the worst possible case.

'Duc,' she stumbled. 'No.'

She couldn't keep the emotion out of her voice or the tears from pooling in her eyes.

She heard him suck in a deep breath, it was almost like he'd flicked a switch somehow. 'I need you,' he repeated. 'There was a car accident. I've had to fly back to Hanoi. We don't have another obstetrician, and I don't have any midwives. I can't do this, Viv. I can't do any of this. I need someone with me. I need someone to help me. Can you come?'

So many questions crowded her brain. She knew there were good, reliable medics who worked at the hospitals. Khiem and Hoa were meticulous about who they hired. But she also knew that, right now, that wasn't what Duc needed to hear.

Officially, she should give notice to her current employer. She hated to be thought of as unreliable. But this was an emergency. A family emergency, because Duc felt like family to her.

'I'll sort it. I'll get there.' As she started pushing random clothes into a bag her heart ached for him. Last

time they'd spoken, a few weeks ago, he'd been full of
enthusiasm. He'd started a new job a month before—a
surgical and teaching fellowship in one of big cities in
the US. She'd almost been a tiny bit jealous about how
happy he'd sounded. Duc had a charm about him, he
was friendly and good at his job. No matter where they'd
worked together in the past, she'd always ridden a little on his coattails. Duc was the one who made friends
and got them invites to dinner and parties. Viv was just
his plus one. It was like he'd realised early on that she
struggled with forming relationships, and he would do
that part for her.

'Thank you,' his voice croaked.

It halted her in her tracks and she dropped back down
onto her knees.

'Of course,' she said without question. 'I'll go to the
airport. I'll find a flight. I'll text you once I have the
details.'

She wanted to wrap her hands around his neck right
now and give him the biggest bear hug. She wanted to
breathe in the, oh, so familiar aftershave that always
drifted into her senses when they were close. She hated
to think of her friend in pain.

'Duc?' she whispered, before she hung up. She looked
at the crooked little finger on her right hand. Years ago
they'd adopted a quirky move from a kids movie where
they intertwined their pinkies and said the phrase,
'Friends for life.' It had become a long-standing joke
between them. She licked her lips. 'Friends for life,' she
said huskily, then her voice broke.

There was a muted pause for a few seconds. This
time he sounded a little stronger. 'Friends for life,' he
repeated, before she hung up the phone.

CHAPTER TWO

DESPITE LEAVING LONDON three days ago, Vivienne still wasn't here.

It could only happen to her. There had been no direct flights available, so she'd taken a whole host of journeys that had bounced her halfway around the globe in order to reach him. She'd had delays, cancellations, engine failure and then an air traffic control strike to contend with. Duc stared at his watch, his eyes flicking back to the arrivals doors at Hanoi airport. Each text had seemed just a little more frantic than the one before.

His stomach was clenched in an uncomfortable knot. It had been this way since he'd got the initial news about his mother and father. He could barely remember packing up his rented apartment, or his flight from Philadelphia to Hanoi. By the time he'd reached the May Mắn Hospital and Lien and her new husband had rushed out to meet him, he had been numb.

There had been a string of traditions and rites around the funeral to take care of. So many people had visited that Duc felt as if he'd worn his white funeral clothes for three days straight. He knew it was because people wanted to pay their respects but keeping his expression in place had been hard.

In the meantime, the hospital had to be kept running. The staff were distraught. The leaders and motivators that they'd worked with for years were gone, and he could see everyone look at him with wariness in their eyes.

By the time he'd buried his mother and father he'd been exhausted. What he really wanted to do was climb back onto a plane and forget anything like this had ever happened. He'd spent the last week hoping someone would pinch him in an on-call room and this whole thing would just have been some kind of monumental nightmare.

Something flickered at the side of his vision. Then a sound. It started as a tinkling laugh that grew into something much deeper and heartier.

His heart gave a little leap. There was only one person who had a laugh like that.

Even though he was tall, he stood on tiptoe to try and catch his first glimpse of her in amongst the exiting crowds.

There. Vivienne was talking animatedly to a rather frail, elderly gentleman, her arm interlinked through his. Her red curls were tumbling down her back in loose waves, a white shirt knotted at her waist and a pair of cut-off denim shorts showing off her long legs.

The original pretty woman. It was what everyone said as soon as they looked at her. Only her Scottish accent betrayed her similarities to the famous actress.

He could see heads turn as she sauntered past. Her casual grace was always noticeable. There weren't too many people here who looked like Viv.

Duc watched as she guided the man over towards his family, walking easily with him as if she had known him all her life. She was in nurse mode. He could tell. People watching would think it was a grandfather and granddaughter, not just some random Scots girl who'd befriended the elderly man on the flight to make sure he was okay. Duc couldn't help the smile that tugged at the edges of his lips—the first time he'd smiled in days. Only Vivienne. He watched as she brought the man safely to his family, shaking hands with them all, before turning around and scanning the crowd until finally catching Duc's gaze.

She didn't hesitate. Her face lit up. She dropped her bags at her feet and ran over to him, jumping up and winding her legs around him. She didn't even say a word. She just buried her face deep into his neck and held on tight.

He could see the amused glances from people close by—as if they were witnessing a pair of lovers reunited. But somehow Duc didn't feel the urge to explain. Just the press of her body against his felt good.

He closed his eyes for a second too and just held her there, letting the heat from her body sink into his. His senses were flooded as the familiar aroma of orange blossom from her shampoo drifted around him.

For an instant in time he was in an entirely different place. One where he hadn't received the call about his parents when he was about to walk into surgery. One where he hadn't had to come here and bury the mother and father he'd unrealistically thought would probably live for ever. One where his current career plans weren't up in the air as he was left with a number of hospitals to run.

Nope. He was in a bubble. A Vivienne-sized bubble. The things he'd craved in the last few days swept over him. Reassurance. Safety. The ability to just be Duc, instead of the bereaved son putting on a brave face— that was the range of feelings that overwhelmed him. Viv was here. She would help him. She would help him sort all this out and get back to the life he truly wanted.

He blinked back the tears that flooded into his eyes. He'd waited days to do this. To feel his friend in his arms and know that someone would have his back. Part of him wished they could teleport out of this airport and straight back to his room so he could crumple on the sofa.

His back was stiff and every muscle in his body ached from keeping it together. He'd nodded his head so many times it was now almost on autopilot. He'd shaken hands with so many old and familiar faces. But for some reason it hadn't brought the comfort he'd thought it would.

This was what he needed. That was what he'd craved.

She pulled her head up, her pale blue eyes just inches from his. 'I stink,' she whispered. 'I've been wearing the same clothes for three days.' She jumped down.

Instantly, his bubble was gone.

'I've smelled worse.' He smiled as he grabbed one of her cases and she slid her arm through his.

As soon as they stepped outside into the warm humid air of Hanoi, Viv started fanning herself. Her brow creased. 'Was it this hot the last time we came here?'

'Hotter,' he replied. He had a car waiting for them outside the airport building and he opened the door for her and waited until she slid inside. He bent his head inside. 'And we need to discuss your clothing.' He winked and pointed at her long bare legs. 'Those? They're a banquet for the mosquitos around here.'

He closed the door and walked around to the other side, climbing in, closing the door and letting her lean back against the cool leather seats. The air-conditioning was on full blast.

'Wait until you get to the hospital. There's a new guy. He was a GP from Scotland. You two will be able to cackle away to each other in Glaswegian, and no one else will have a clue what you're saying.'

She turned her head and raised one eyebrow—a move Viv had perfected years before. 'Cackle?'

He laughed, something that came from deep inside him. But the release of the laugh made his shoulders shake in a way he couldn't quite work out, then his arms and his hands.

It was almost as if a switch had been flicked somewhere deep down inside. By the time the tears started to fall down his cheeks, Viv had slid across the leather and wrapped her arms around his neck. 'Oh, Duc,' she said quietly, 'what am I going to do with you?'

It wasn't really a question. And he knew that—and was glad, because he couldn't possibly answer it. All the emotions he'd bottled up from the last few days just seemed to come tumbling out.

The frustration. The anger. The grief. All while Vivienne held him and the city sped past outside.

This wasn't what he'd wanted. It had been years since she'd visited Hanoi. He'd expected to point out some of the sights to her, and then talk to her about the current issues at the hospital. He couldn't do that when he was struggling to even breathe.

It was like she read his mind.

'Count to ten,' she whispered in his ear. 'We'll do it together.'

Her voice was slow and steady. 'One, two, three, four, five, six, seven, eight, nine, ten.'

She did it again. Then again.

Each time she slowed her speech down more, making his breaths longer and smoother. One of her hands rubbed his back while the other intertwined her fingers with his.

By the time he realised that the car had stopped outside the May Mǎn Hospital he felt as if he was back to normal—or as normal as he could feel.

He ran one hand through his hair and shook his head, almost embarrassed to look Viv in the eye. This was the last thing he wanted to do.

'I'm sorry,' he said hoarsely.

'Why?' she said simply, as she moved back over to the other side of the car and picked up her bag. 'I'm your best friend. If you can't be like this with me, then who can you be like this with?'

She opened the door before he had a chance to say anything else, stretching out her back and facing the pale yellow hospital. 'Now,' she said loudly in her no-nonsense Scottish accent, 'before anything else—can you show me where the shower is?'

And for the first time in days things finally felt as if they might be a bit better.

CHAPTER THREE

SHE'D SPENT THE last three nights sleeping on chairs or airport floors. Every bone and muscle in her body ached.

The hospital was eerily quiet. The staff she'd met had shaken hands with her politely and looked at Duc with wary eyes. She could sense everyone tiptoeing around him.

She'd always loved this place on the times they'd visited. Even the name May Mắn, which translated to 'good luck' in English and that was what she always called it in her head. The Good Luck Hospital. The place had an upbeat vibe and served one of the poorest populations in Hanoi. But somehow now, as they passed through the corridors, the vibe felt very different.

Once they'd walked through to the grounds at the back, he took her to one of the three white cottages built on the land the hospital owned. It had a pale yellow door. Khiem and Hoa's house.

For some strange reason she hadn't thought he would be staying in his parents' home and it made her catch her breath.

She blinked. Unexpected tears formed in her eyes. She'd met Khiem and Hoa on a few occasions. They had been lovely, warm people, dedicated to their work, and to the people they'd served.

She'd been able to tell from a few glances just how proud they had been of their son. But more than that, they'd been welcoming, interested in the lonely Scottish girl that Duc had invited into their home. They'd never made her feel as if she'd outstayed her welcome, or that she couldn't come back whenever she wanted. Hoa had emailed on a few occasions when vacancies had arisen at the hospital—almost giving Viv first refusal. It had been considerate, and kind, and she'd appreciated the gesture, even though she'd only ever visited with Duc.

Now she was back in their home, without really having had time to mourn the passing of her friends. She'd missed the funeral and just walking through the front door sent her senses into overload.

She glanced nervously at Duc, wondering what this must be doing to him. Today was the first time in their friendship that she'd ever seen him break down.

Of course he would. He'd just lost his mum and dad in some random crazy car accident. And deep inside she knew that it had killed him to do that in front of her. But this was why she'd come. This was why she hadn't hesitated to jump on a plane to get here.

Duc had played this role in her life over and over again. By the time they'd met, her adoptive parents had already died. He'd supported her when she'd searched for her birth parents—and had been there when both of them had turned out to be less than she'd hoped for. He'd wrapped her in his arms when she'd had her heart broken twice. And when she'd had a cruel diagnosis a few years ago that had messed with her head.

Of course she would be here for him. Her heart was

breaking for him—but she wouldn't let him see that. Here, she had to be the strong one. Duc had played the role for her time and time again, and this time she would do it for him.

Even if everything in this quaint house reminded her in every way of both his parents.

She breathed deeply. She could even smell them here—the jasmine tea they always drank, the sandalwood cologne his father always wore, and the rose-scented spray his mother used in the rooms. Vivienne blinked. The truth was that she expected them to walk through the door at any moment. And if she felt like that, she could only imagine how Duc was feeling.

She reached over and grabbed his hand. 'Duc, are you sure about staying here? About being here?'

On a table was a framed picture of Duc and his parents together. In another corner was a pile of books that one of his parents must have been reading. A popular fiction novel, a historical romance, a book about alternative therapies and a research journal about obstetrics.

He turned around to look at her, leaving her case in the middle of the sitting room. For the first time she realised just how tired he looked. 'Where else can I go? I've have to cover shifts at the hospital.' He looked almost apologetic. 'And so do you.'

She nodded. 'Of course. I'm ready to start tomorrow. Just tell me what you need me to do.' She gave him a careful stare. 'There isn't anywhere else you can stay but here?'

He looked around and held out his hands. 'Here,' he said. 'It's home. It's not my home,' he said quickly, 'but it's theirs. And I can't stay anywhere else.'

He stepped forward and tugged her case. 'I've put you

in here. I changed the beds...' He pulled a face. 'Actually, that's not true. Mai Ahn, our interpreter, came in and did everything. I think she just wanted to help and, to be honest, I'm really glad she did.'

He was accepting help. Good. Duc could be stubborn sometimes, his intense pride getting in the way of things. She wasn't sure quite what kind of relationship he had with the people who worked here, but at least he wasn't shutting everyone out.

Viv moved towards the room. It only took an instant to realise the room had belonged to Khiem and Hoa. Their belongings were still scattered at various points around the place. A pair of shoes neatly tucked under a chair. Another book on the bedside table. A notepad with some scribbles next to the phone in the room. She gulped, feeling a little overwhelmed. Of course she could object—but Duc was obviously using the other room. Objecting would just make things more difficult for him.

She pressed her lips together for a second then turned and gave him a bright smile. 'Okay, let me get showered, then we can talk.'

There was the briefest of pauses. Talking was the last thing Duc clearly wanted to do. But she wasn't going to be put off. She was here to help, and she couldn't do that by not talking. Duc knew her better than that anyhow.

She walked back over and stood underneath his nose. 'No, I'm not too tired. No, I don't want to do anything else first. Find me some food, and I'm all yours.' She nudged him with her elbow. 'No excuses.'

He let out a sigh. It was clear she'd won this battle. 'No excuses,' he agreed as he strode through to the kitchen and started opening cupboards.

* * *

He hadn't eaten properly in the last three days. He hadn't been hungry, and it had been the last thing on his mind. But as he pulled some food from the cupboards and fridge, splashed some oil into the wok, his stomach let out an involuntary rumble.

He heard the sound of the running shower, closely followed by the blast of the hairdryer. Vivienne was quick, opening the door with her hair in a red cloud around her head and wearing a pair of soft white cotton pyjamas. She glanced towards the table and tiled floor, then moved across to the sofa and sagged down on the comfortable cushions, pulling her feet up. Duc was already serving up into two bowls. He handed her the chicken and noodle mixture then sat down next to her on the sofa.

She warily sniffed her dish. 'Okay, is this edible?'

He smiled. 'What are you trying to say about my cooking?'

'I say that for as long as I've known you, your cooking has always involved a takeout menu.'

He pretended to look hurt. 'Try it. It's one of my mother's recipes.'

The words came out of nowhere, quickly followed by the tumbleweed that seemed to blow across the room in front of him.

Viv's hand reached over and gave his knee a quick squeeze. 'I'm sure it's fine,' she said quietly, as she started to eat.

Every spoonful was an unconscious reminder. He'd used the spices and oils from his mother's cupboards. The pangs of hunger he'd felt for a few moments instantly vanished. Now he understood why grieving friends lost weight. It was so easy to be distracted—to be put off.

Vivienne was different—she ate hungrily, emptying the bowl in five minutes. She stood up and walked over to the fridge, examining the contents before pulling out a bottle of spring water. 'This wasn't what I had in mind,' she said as she held it up, 'but I'll make do.'

He watched as she rested one hand on the chair. Her white cotton pyjamas might cover every part of her, but they still highlighted every curve. Curves he'd never really paid any attention to before—and he was currently asking himself why.

The lines between him and Vivienne had been clear from the beginning. They were friends—best friends. He'd held her hair back while she'd been sick, she'd put him up when his roommate had wrecked their apartment and they'd been flung out. From the word *go*, they'd felt comfortable around each other. They'd had countless conversations over the years about Viv's disastrous relationships. She was smart. She was gorgeous. She was sassy. And she had appalling taste in men.

Every no-good layabout, sob-story-carrying wastrel seemed to cross her path. Each one breaking her heart more than the one before.

Viv had also cast her eyes over Duc's partners over the years. Some she'd been grudgingly approving of, others had been dismissed with a wave of a hand and a few perceptive words. *Gold-digger. Stalker. Needs a backbone. Self-obsessed.*

He, in turn, grudgingly admitted that on most occasions those few words had turned out to be uncannily accurate. He'd started to call her the fortune teller and tease her to pick their lottery numbers.

But she hadn't seen this coming.

The door rattled behind them and Lien burst through the door. 'Good, you're here. I need you.'

Lien's eyes went hastily to Vivienne and she gave a little start.

Duc stepped forward. 'Lien, this is Vivienne Kerr, my friend, the midwife that I told you about.'

Lien gave a quick nod of her head. 'Perfect timing.' She didn't ask why Vivienne was standing in Duc's house in her pyjamas. Instead she turned back to the door. 'Get changed quickly—you're needed.'

Everything happened in the blink of an eye. One minute Viv was contemplating sitting down with her friend and finding out exactly how she could help him best.

The next second she was stripping off her comfortable PJs and yanking on a pair of the burgundy-coloured scrubs she kept in the top of her rucksack. She grabbed her matching soft shoes and ran across the grass, back towards the hospital.

Even though it was the middle of the night, every corridor was brightly lit. Vivienne followed the others. Lien was talking rapidly in Vietnamese and Duc was nodding. She tried to focus. She'd worked here a few times and had picked up a few phrases in Vietnamese. For a midwife they mainly comprised of 'push', 'stop' and 'breathe', but her brain was struggling to remember them right now.

Duc walked through to another room. Viv tried to keep track. She hadn't familiarised herself completely with this place again. Between that, the jet-lag, and the overwhelming sweep of tiredness, she wasn't firing on all cylinders. Thank goodness she'd had time to eat.

Her hands caught her hair and coiled it at the back of her neck, twisting it back on itself until it was anchored in place. Lien's gaze caught hers. 'Neat trick.' She gave Viv an anxious smile.

Viv shrugged. 'Years of people stealing my hair elastics. Had to improvise.'

The anxiousness of Lien's smile made Viv's stomach clench. Last time Viv had been here she'd been impressed by the relaxed nature of most of the deliveries at May Mắn Hospital. Hoa had very much believed in letting the woman take the lead for her labour—much like most of the midwife-led units back home—and Viv shared this philosophy. But right now? When there was a clinical emergency? Things were different. Now it was the job of the professionals to guide the woman and baby to the safest possible conclusion, and from the look on Lien's face it was up to Viv to take the lead.

Duc pulled his T-shirt over his head, swapping it for a pale blue scrub top that he grabbed from the pile on a rack on the wall. Viv tried not to stare. But it had been a long time since she'd seen Duc in a state of semi-undress. His chiselled abs weren't lost on her. She wasn't blind. She pulled her eyes away just as Lien moved closer. 'Do you want to come and meet our patient, Viv?'

Viv nodded. 'Of course.'

Lien gave her a small smile as she pushed open a door. 'I'll introduce you.'

Lien gestured to the woman in the bed. There was another man with light brown hair by her bed. 'This is Resta. She's thirty-nine weeks, or thereabouts. Presented in labour with what appears to be shoulder dystocia. We have no prenatal history.'

Viv nodded. Because she'd worked here before with

Duc she knew it wasn't entirely unusual for women not to present for prenatal care.

Lien pointed to the other guy in the room. 'My husband, Dr Joe Lennox.'

Joe was in position at the bottom of the bed, one hand cradling part of the baby's head. He gave a quick glance up. 'I hope you're the cavalry,' he said in a hushed voice, keeping his expression neutral, 'because I'm no obstetrician and I'm out of options.' His Glasgow accent was thick, and Viv immediately recognised the stress in his voice.

Viv drew in a breath. Shoulder dystocia. Every midwife and obstetrician's nightmare. A baby whose shoulder got stuck and stopped the baby being delivered safely.

Viv looked around the room quickly, locating some gloves. 'Would you like me to take a look?'

Joe nodded gratefully. 'Please.' Lien turned to the woman on the bed and spoke to her in Vietnamese, introducing Vivienne to her. There was no getting away from it, the woman looked exhausted and terrified. No wonder. Shoulder dystocia could rarely be predicted. Women typically got to the end of a long labour and once they'd delivered their baby's head thought it was only a matter of minutes until it was all over.

Vivienne glanced around the room again, quickly taking note of the equipment available to her.

She took a deep breath. Lien and Joe were both doing their best to keep their faces neutral, but Joe had already told her this wasn't his field. From what she'd gathered from Duc, this was nobody's field right now at May Mắn Hospital.

Hoa was dead, and the other obstetrician who normally helped out was off sick, having just been diagnosed with breast cancer.

It looked like Vivienne was the total of midwifery and obstetric knowledge here.

She could see the baby's head tight against the perineum. This wasn't the first time she'd dealt with a shoulder dystocia. But usually a diagnosis was followed by hitting the emergency buzzer, with two other midwives, an anaesthetist and an obstetrician all rushing to assist.

Those people weren't here now. It was her. It was just her.

Deep inside, part of her wanted to scream for this poor woman. She'd worked with Duc over the years, and she knew he was a good doctor. The absolute worst-case scenario here would be the Zavanelli manoeuvre, where they had to try and put the baby's head back into the vagina and perform an emergency caesarean section. Duc was the only surgeon here. She doubted if he'd performed a caesarean section before but, if need be, she could talk him through it.

She pushed that thought away and tried not to think about it, taking a note of the time on the clock on the wall.

Viv moved automatically into midwife mode, reassuring her patient, even though she didn't speak the language, and letting Lien or Duc take time to translate everything she said.

It was a stressful situation for everyone in the room. Joe and Lien were calm influences, moving smoothly and easily. They seemed to foresee each other's actions. It was interesting to watch them work together.

Vivienne took charge. Assessing her patient. Directing her not to push. She attached a monitor to the baby that would alert her to any signs of distress.

'Okay, folks,' she said calmly. 'We're going to try a change of position. It's called the McRoberts manoeuvre and it's used in this condition to try and release the shoulder. What we really want to do is create some space in the pelvis, and we need to move mum and, sometimes, baby to do that.'

She gave Lien a nod, waiting for her to explain to Resta that they were going to help her to lie on her back and move her legs outwards and up towards her chest. As this was a delivery room there was no end on the bed and Vivienne could move easily to try and assist.

She kept her face completely neutral. 'This entirely depends on the baby's position. If it's the anterior shoulder caught under the symphysis pubis, this tends to work.'

'And if it's not?' Duc's dark eyes met hers. He'd moved behind the patient, supporting her position.

Vivienne kept her voice calm and low. 'If it's both shoulders, they'll be stuck under the pelvis brim and this won't help. But this is where we start.'

She kept calm. Running through the mental checklist in her head. Waiting to see if the change of position would have any effect on the baby's ability to be delivered. She was lucky. This baby wasn't showing signs of distress. Yet.

After a few minutes she shifted to the side of the bed, giving Duc a nod. 'I'm going to press on the abdomen just above the pubic bone to try and release the shoulder. Can someone explain to Resta and keep reassuring her?'

Duc nodded and spoke in a deep, low voice, his hand gently on the woman's arm. She could tell that the woman seemed to trust what he was telling her, even though she was clearly exhausted. Viv understood that at this stage all any woman wanted was to deliver her baby and have it safely in her arms.

It was interesting. She was in a room with three doctors, who were all perfectly willing to allow her to take the lead. There were no power struggles in here. Everyone just wanted this baby out safely.

Vivienne kept a careful eye on the clock and the baby monitor. Timing was crucial.

'Okay, time to try something else, I'm going to do something called the Rubin manoeuvre to try and release the baby's shoulders.'

She explained carefully, then slid fingers in on either side of the baby's head, trying a number of techniques, without success.

The baby's heart rate started to slow. Both mum and baby were tired, and the baby was starting to get distressed.

She was calm and methodical, secretly glad that the heart monitor wasn't on her instead of the baby because, despite everything, panic was definitely setting in. She wasn't quite sure how long it would take them to set up a theatre if need be.

'Okay,' she said. The baby's head was still wedged tightly, with very little room for a blade to make an episiotomy. 'Let's try mum around on all fours. Let's see if a further change of position lets things move on.'

In another few minutes she would need to attempt to deliver one of the baby's arms or give Duc the nod that they needed to head to Theatre. She was running out of options.

Lien explained in a reassuring manner to Resta what

they wanted her to try, just as Vivienne sent a little prayer skyward. Joe and Duc helped mum around and baby let out a little grumble at the change of position.

But within a few seconds it was clear it was the right move. Resta was on all fours on the bed. Viv hated the fact she no longer had eye contact with mum, but this was a case of needs must.

Almost instantly she could see a change. 'Give me a second,' she said to the others. The baby's face looked a little more relaxed. 'I think the shoulder's been dislodged. Tell Resta to give me a push on her next contraction.'

One minute later the little bundle slid out into her arms. After a few seconds of shocked silence the baby started screaming. Vivienne did a few quick checks. Colour was good. Baby was breathing.

Joe appeared at her side and held out his hands for the baby. Duc helped her clamp and cut the cord, then they helped Resta turn back around to deliver the placenta. Viv caught Joe's eye. He gave a hopeful nod. When shoulder dystocia had a complicated delivery there could be injuries to the baby's shoulders and nerves. The baby would need to be observed. But for now he brought the baby over to let mum have a cuddle. *Đó là một cô gái,'* he said.

A girl. She recognised the word. Mum looked thrilled. The relief in the room was palpable, all the professionals exchanging glances. Duc shot her a smile and gave a grateful nod of his head as he walked back towards her. 'Thank goodness you were here,' he whispered.

Viv looked around the room as she started to tidy up. 'I'm sure you would have all got there.' The clenching in her stomach was only just starting to ease.

Lien came over and rubbed Viv's arm. 'Thanks so much.' She glanced at her husband. 'Sorry for the rude introduction earlier. Joe and I can take it from here. You must be exhausted.'

Viv nodded. 'I am, but let me finish the notes and a few final checks on mum.' It didn't matter how tired she was. She would always make sure her clinical work and her paperwork were completed.

One of the aides brought in some jasmine tea, and Joe did some more checks on the baby. As Vivienne made sure she was satisfied that mum and baby were settled and well cared for, Duc slung an arm around her shoulders.

'You look as if you haven't slept in a week. Let's go. Those jammies are still waiting.'

They walked back out into the cooler night air. Viv stopped for a moment, putting her hands on her hips and arching her aching back.

'Okay?' He was right next to her, the warmth from his body crossing the minuscule space between them.

She looked up into his dark eyes. 'You weren't joking, were you—when you said you'd no one for obstetrics?'

His dark eyes clouded. He shook his head. 'No. No one. I don't know when, or if, our other doctor will be back. This was an area that my mother always took care of—was always on top of. The last few days...' he looked up the dark night sky '...I guess we've just been lucky.'

'You can't rely on luck, Duc,' she said quickly. 'That's not fair on the staff, or the patients.'

He sighed, and she could literally see the energy sagging out of his body. He'd come into that situation to-night, knowing that performing an unfamiliar surgery could be the difference between life and death for that mum and baby. She hadn't seen him halt or contemplate refusing. He'd been there. Ready to perform if required.

She turned to face him, their bodies almost touching. 'What would have happened if you'd needed to do a section?'

He paused for only a second. 'Then I would have done a section.' He looked down at her. 'I'm sure you could have talked me through it.'

Viv's skin prickled—and not in a good way. 'But that puts horrible pressure on you, and me.' She shook her head. 'This can't happen again.'

He stepped back and ran his hands through his hair. 'You think I don't know that?' He threw his hands upwards. 'You think I wasn't in there absolutely crapping myself?' He turned his back and took a few steps away from her, his momentary flare of anger starting to dissipate. 'You think I want any of this, Viv?'

His voice broke and she stepped forward and took his hands in hers. He kept talking. 'Of course I don't. But tonight would have been considered emergency surgery. Whether obstetrics is my area or not, I'm still a general surgeon. I would still be expected to perform emergency surgery as and when required.'

His hands were shaking, and she realised just how scared he had actually been.

'I don't want to be here, Viv. I don't want any of this. But what can I do? The worst part about all this—I don't even feel myself right now. I can't be myself. I need to be Khiem and Hoa's son.' He had a bit of a wild, panicked look in his eyes. 'The one who will sort out the hospitals and make sure the patients are looked after. The one who will make sure everything keeps running exactly as it did before—supplying all the same services for patients, even though we're two doctors down. Maybe I just wave my magic wand and whip them out of thin air? I tried to place an advert and begin the recruitment process yesterday—but apparently there's some red tape and I need to meet with the lawyer first. How can a hospital run with no doctors?'

He put his hands on his hips and took a few deep breaths, his head downcast. Now she understood the pressure he was truly under. Before, she'd just been thinking about the grief of losing his parents. But it seemed she really should have paid much more attention to his panicked phone call. He raised his head and met her gaze, pressing a hand to his chest. 'I can't just be Duc Nguyen, surgeon from Philadelphia. The guy who was just about to sign on a house he's spent the last six months looking for. The guy who had been tipped that he was going to be offered the next slot on the team at the teaching hospital. I'd even been told to start thinking about recruiting my own team.' He threw up his hands. 'This is just not where I thought I would be.'

She reached over and put her hand on his arm, gently bringing it back down. Part of her had always envied Duc and his lovely family life. But now she could see how much pain it had unlocked for him. Maybe her detached way of life was actually easier.

She hadn't known about the house, or the potential to become a permanent member of the team in Philadelphia. That was huge. He must have done so well. It was clear they were impressed by him. Now she understood exactly how much being here was costing him.

He closed his eyes and spoke quietly. 'The reading of the will is in a few days and then I'll find out what my parents' plans were for this place.' His face crumpled.

'They always mentioned they wanted me to take over—and I always told them my heart was in surgery. But we never had a truly serious conversation—not one with plans and lawyers. Our half-hearted discussions took place at the dinner table or between seeing patients when I came back and helped out during the holidays. Now I'm realising how much I don't know. I guess we just never imagined that something like this would happen.'

He shook his head. 'Until it did.' He held out his hands for a few seconds, before walking closer and resting them down on her shoulders.

His head dipped towards hers. And they stood there for a few seconds in the moonlight with their foreheads touching. 'I'm just glad you're here, Viv. I couldn't cope with any of this without you.'

She had so much she wanted to say right now—about the hospital, the responsibilities, the issues that needed to be sorted out straight away. But it wasn't the time. He didn't need that right now. What Duc needed right now was his friend.

She reached up and put her hand over his, giving it a squeeze. 'And you don't need to.'

They stood for a few more moments, before Duc slung his arm back around her shoulders and they walked back to the bungalow.

As he pushed open the door, he gave her a half-smile. 'Hey, Viv?'

She was already eyeing her discarded white pyjamas, dying to jump straight back into them. She glanced back at him. 'What?'

He gave her a weary smile. 'Welcome to Hanoi.'

CHAPTER FOUR

VIVIENNE HAD WORKED in a lot of places. She generally lasted between six months and a year before moving on. She made friends superficially at each new workplace. She was good at her job and generally had a good feel for people—she naturally knew who to avoid and who to trust. Her instincts had always been sound—except, of course, when it came to men.

Viv seemed to have an inbuilt ability to find the worst man in the room—no matter where she was. Her love life had been one disaster after another. The only guy that had been half-good was Archie, an electrician she'd met when she'd worked in Bristol. Archie had been too good, too nice—even Duc had liked him. But Archie had got too close. He'd tried to support her when she'd tried to trace her birth mum and then found out she was dead. His sympathy had felt overwhelming. His questions about how she was feeling had probed into emotions she wasn't ready to deal with. It was almost like he had been trying to 'fix her'—and Viv didn't need to be fixed by anyone.

So she'd done what she did best, and retreated quickly. Instead, seeking out men who were their own natural disasters, and emotionally unavailable to her, made her life simpler. It made it easier to keep the shell she'd constructed around herself unbroken. Duc was the only person who'd ever been allowed to tap at the surface—the only man she'd ever really trusted. Which was why she was here, trying to get her head around her role within this hospital.

By day three she'd begun to get a feel for the place again. May Mắn Hospital had always been a little different. She'd only been here for short spells, but there was something about this place—it had a little buzz around it that she couldn't explain. Before, she'd just imagined it was because of the connection to Duc. His parents had always been the heart and soul of the place.

Walking through the corridors, she could almost sense the echo of them. She half expected to turn a corner and walk into either one of them.

Trouble was, the staff had relied on them so much for, well, everything.

Lien seemed to have a good head on her shoulders for the day-to-day running of the hospital. For the general medical patients she was the go-to clinician. But she didn't know anything about rotas, ordering supplies, or maintenance of the building. Her husband, Joe, helped out at some of the antenatal clinics. He'd worked as a GP back in Scotland, and could do general antenatal care, as well as regular hospital duties. But what was most interesting was the fact he seemed to have a real panache for working with the kids. They seemed to gravitate towards him—even though he still struggled with the language barrier, much the same as she did. It probably helped that he had a young son of his own, but watching her colleagues gave Viv a chance to understand the skills of those around her.

While all that was well and good, she hadn't found anyone who had the skills she needed as an obstetrician. There was a visiting plastic surgeon, there was Duc, and there was a whole host of part-time nurses working within the hospital.

Trouble was that between Hoa and the other obstetrician there really had been no one else to look after the steady stream of pregnant women who came to the hospital. Viv had learned quickly that not all women in Hanoi presented early enough in their pregnancy to have any kind of antenatal screening.

Viv was lucky. One of her jobs had been on a Scottish island and had required her to have further training in carrying out sonograms. This meant she found herself doing routine sonograms on a whole range of women at different gestations, coming up against a whole host of potential issues.

The truth was, she couldn't do this on her own. She was a midwife. Not a consultant.

She wandered through the corridors in the midst of another busy day. Duc was sitting at the desk in her father's office, his head resting on one hand.

'Knock, knock,' she said as she walked in.

He looked up. There were dark circles under his eyes. Even though she knew he went to bed at night, it was clear he wasn't sleeping.

He started to stand up but she shook her head as she sat in the chair opposite him. 'Don't. There's no emergency. But we need to talk.'

His brow creased. 'Just don't tell me you're leaving.'

She gave a weak smile. 'Not yet. But you know me. I never hang my hat anywhere for long.'

He opened his mouth as if he was about to respond, then shook his head and held out one hand. 'So, what's up?'

She nodded. This was business. It had to be. She could see gaps that she wasn't comfortable working around.

'Things need to be clearer. At any other hospital I've worked at, we have protocols. A strict set of guidelines that everyone follows for certain events, certain conditions.' She gave him a weak smile. 'Thing is, at May Mắn? The protocols were your mum—literally. She knew everything, and everyone just went on her say-so. While that was fine when she was here...'

Duc winced and she cringed at her choice of words, but Viv kept going, this was too important. 'Now... she's not. Staff need guidelines to work to. Written-down guidelines. Maybe even stuck-to-the-wall guidelines. Your mother and Dr Tan were their safety net. Not all the nurses are midwives here. Some of them don't know the first thing about dealing with maternity patients. In lots of cases the care isn't difficult. They just need specifics. What to do, what to look out for, when to raise the alarm.' She paused for a second, letting her words sink in.

Part of her was amazed at herself. She never really stayed anywhere long enough to look at procedures and protocols. Last time she'd been here, she'd been just as guilty of using Hoa as her sounding board. But Hoa wasn't here now, and staff were unsure.

'This could be relatively simple. There are protocols and guidelines for most things in hospitals the world over. We can choose the ones that work here, and you can get someone to help me translate them. The staff can do short training sessions, and we can put the most important ones in easy, visible places as reminders.'

Duc put his head in his hands. He was shaking it. 'I can't believe something so basic isn't in place.' He glanced back up, an incredulous look on his face. 'How come this wasn't done before?'

Viv pressed her lips together. It wasn't up to her to judge. She'd no right to. She was just an outsider here. All she knew was that some of the staff were out of their depth and dealing with cases that stretched their abilities. They didn't have the back-up that was normally in place.

'We need some safeguards.' She put her hand on her chest. 'And I need some safeguards. Have you thought about getting another obstetrician, or at least another midwife?'

Duc sighed. 'Of course. But my hands have been tied with red tape that I don't understand. I am so out of my depth I don't even know which way to turn.' He held up both hands. 'This?' He looked around. 'This was just a place to come and help out. Do a few ward rounds, pre-scribe some antibiotics, help with the occasional clinic. Cover the on-call so my mum and dad could have a few nights together.' He leaned back in his chair. 'What I know about obstetrics I could write on the back of a postage stamp. I've spent the last two days panic-reading about emergency caesarean sections just in case it hap-pens in the next few days.'

He shook his head. 'Have you any idea how long it takes to advertise a post, check someone's credentials, then wait for them to give notice at a previous post?'

Vivienne leaned across the desk towards him, put her head on her hand and raised one eyebrow, obviously waiting for the penny to drop.

After the briefest of seconds Duc realised what he'd

said. 'Yeah, sorry about that. Did I wreck your chances of ever getting another job with that health authority?'

Vivienne sat back and gave a half-hearted shrug. Truth was, she'd quite liked the place where she'd been working. The staff were pleasant enough, and she'd managed to rent a flat in a nice area. A flat that was now currently empty. Maybe she was getting old. It was the first time she'd ever really thought like that. 'You know me,' she answered flippantly. 'Only take one job per health authority then I move on.'

'Keep that up and you'll eventually run out,' said Duc. He was watching her carefully.

'That's why every now and then I throw a whole different country into the mix.' She leaned right back and put her feet up on the table. 'I was contemplating Ireland next. Probably Dublin. Anyway, I told my boss it was an unexpected family emergency. I might have left them in the lurch a little, but I'd just finished two weeks on call—and that's definitely not allowed. I'd bent over backwards to help them cover shifts, and I worked hard.'

Duc's eyes clouded a little. 'Family,' he said softly.

Vivienne gulped. 'That's what we are,' she said simply. 'At least, that's what I think we are.'

She meant it. Getting into midwifery college at seventeen had been a blessing. A year later her adoptive parents had died and when she'd tried to track down her birth parents it hadn't exactly been good news. Her birth mother had died from cancer years earlier and her father had spent his life in and out of prison. She didn't have any idea where he was right now. When she'd qualified at age twenty, she'd taken every opportunity that had come her way.

Her salary was enough to rent somewhere reasonable

in whatever city she took a job—some of the hospitals even had staff accommodation at reduced rates. Duc had been the one reliable, relatable friend she'd made along the way. Her ground level. The person she spoke to most. The person she always connected to.

It was odd. Although they'd visited before, she was now seeing Duc in a completely new light. It was clear he'd never seen himself as an integral part of May Mắn hospital. His career aspirations had never been here. He'd always been focused on being a surgeon.

But now? With his parents dead, she did wonder if he might reconsider.

Duc gave her a sad smile. 'Family. Yeah. It's just you and me now. Maybe you should reconsider, I don't know if I'm that lucky right now.'

He stood up, pushing his chair back, and headed for the door. As he reached the doorway he paused and looked back at her. The circles under his eyes were so dark. He was still hurting. Of course he was. She was supposed to be here to take some of the burden. Instead, she'd just come in and heaped a whole lot of trouble on top of him. What kind of a friend was she really?

'After the will reading tomorrow,' he said slowly, 'I'll get to some of this stuff. I will. I promise.'

He looked as though the weight of the world was on his shoulders. Tears brimmed in her eyes. She gave a stiff nod.

He'd just lost both parents. How on earth could she expect him to think straight? If she really wanted to be a friend, she was going to have to step up.

CHAPTER FIVE

THE LAWYER'S OFFICE was unfamiliar. It took three attempts to find the correct street. By the time he got there, his shirt was already sticking to his back.

Vivienne had agreed to come with him. She was wearing a thin, pale green long-sleeved blouse and dark skirt and heels—not her normal attire.

As she stepped out of the car, her long red curls swinging, he could see heads turn in her direction. There was something different about a woman's walk when she wore heels. Viv didn't walk. She strode. Every step accentuated the cinch of her waist, the swing of her hips and the curves of her breasts.

His footsteps hesitated and he pushed the thoughts from his head. Nerves. That was what this was. He didn't think about Viv like this.

She moved to his side, fingers touching his arm and her orange blossom scent dancing through the air towards him. 'Are you okay with this?' Her voice was laced with concern.

He sucked in a breath. 'I have to be. What other choice do I have? We just…never had the chance to talk about anything like this.' His feet were rooted to the pavement. The air around him felt oppressive.

Viv moved her hand and interlocked their pinkies in their old trade-mark move. She gave him a soft smile. 'Friends for life,' she whispered.

He nodded, finding her words reassuring. 'Friends for life,' he repeated, and they walked up the stairs to the lawyer's office.

The man was waiting for them. 'Pleasure to meet you, Dr Nguyen. I am just sorry it's under such sad circumstances. I knew your mother and father for many years. I am Henry Quang.'

He had a slight twang of an American accent. 'Have you always worked here in Hanoi?' asked Duc.

He shook his head. 'I have offices in Washington, New York and Hanoi.' Duc nodded. Now he understood why Quang's name seemed Westernised. In normal circumstances he would have introduced himself slightly differently but, as Duc had found himself, constantly explaining why in Vietnam surnames, middles names and forenames came in a different order quickly became wearing.

The man gestured towards the seats across his desk. 'Please, take a seat.'

Duc's stomach gave an uncomfortable flip. This all felt so final. He'd spent most of the last week living in a weird kind of bubble. He kept expecting his parents to walk back through the door. His father to be sitting in his office. His mother to come beaming down the corridor to tell him about a delivery. Or either one of them to be sitting in the kitchen in the bungalow, sorting out medical cover for one of the other hospitals.

Now, sitting in their lawyer's office, he knew things were finally coming to a head. This was it. This was where he had to stop playing make-believe.

'I have to let you know that my mother and father and I never really had a chance to talk about their…plans.'

Quang gave a solemn nod. 'Believe it or not, Mr Nguyen, that isn't unusual. In a way, you're lucky.' He realised what he'd said and lifted one hand, rapidly shaking his head. 'No, I didn't mean it that way at all. What I mean is that your mother and father planned ahead. Because they had responsibility for three different hospitals, they put plans in place.'

Part of him felt relieved. Maybe he'd been wrong to worry about things.

'Okay.'

Viv gave him a kind of forced smile. It seemed he wasn't the only one nervous in here.

The lawyer spread some papers across his desk, spinning them around to face Duc.

'There are a number of properties. The three bungalows in the grounds of May Mắn hospital, the hospital itself. The second hospital in Trà Bồng and the third in Uong Bi. They also have several other properties. An apartment near May Mắn Hospital. A small house in the south of France and an apartment at Canary Wharf in London.'

Duc gave a nod. He knew about all these places.

'Naturally, the ownership of all these properties passes to you, Duc.'

'All of them?' He blinked.

'Yes, as Khiem and Hoa's son and heir, you are the only person named in their will.'

Duc gulped. 'But what about the running of the hospitals? The arrangements? They must have put some provision in place.'

Mr Quang gave a tight-lipped nod. He pulled out a

folder from under his desk. 'Yes, they did leave a number of instructions. Mainly about practical things. Supplies, deliveries, bank accounts. Payroll arrangements and details of their accountant.' He gave a sympathetic smile. 'It is all rather complicated.'

Duc leaned forward, trying to drown out the roaring that was currently in his ears. 'But the hospitals. There has to be some other arrangements. I assumed...' he ran a hand through his hair '...that they'd made some kind of provision—a long term plan. Arrangements for a board of some sort, or an oversight committee.'

Quang shook his head. 'Maybe they hoped you'd change your mind? Or, as you said, they hadn't quite foreseen anything like this happening and assumed they would have plenty of time to put those kinds of arrangements in place.' Quang gave him an almost impertinent look.

'When I said they'd made arrangements, I was talking about the fact they'd even got around to making a will. Have you any idea how many people don't get that far?' He didn't even wait for an answer to that question before continuing, holding up the folder. 'This contains most of the essential information you'll need for the safe running of the hospitals. In most instances this could take months to find.'

He leaned back in his chair but left his hands clasped together on the desk. 'The legalities of everything, the transfer of rights, et cetera, will, inevitably, take some time. Probably a minimum of six months. You won't be able to make any major changes or...' he raised one eyebrow as he looked straight at Duc '...or sales until that point.'

A chill passed over Duc. This really wasn't happening. It just couldn't be.

'But what about staffing? I have no obstetrician. If rights don't pass to me, I'm assuming I can't advertise posts for staff? And what about the bank accounts and payroll—are the staff supposed to work without getting paid?'

The lawyer gave a smile, shook his head and shuffled some papers. 'No, no, of course not. There are legal provisions for situations such as these—when there are hospital or medical facilities involved. Your parents had an agreement with the Vietnamese government about providing medical facilities within areas of greatest need. That allows some…' he pulled a face '…flexibility, in order to allow the service to continue. It falls under…' he lifted his fingers '…"emergency service" remit.'

Duc tried to breathe in—even though it felt as if a clamp had just fastened around his chest. 'That makes sense,' he muttered. He'd heard about similar arrangements in the past.

The lawyer pulled out some other papers. 'You can recruit staff in order to maintain service provision.'

Duc shook his head, waiting to see if Mr Quang would say anything else. But silence filled the space. 'That's it? Six months until the paperwork is sorted out?' He knew his voice was rising in pitch, but he couldn't help it. 'I can't stay here. I have a job—responsibilities. I've currently left a teaching hospital in Philadelphia without a resident surgeon. I'm part of a programme. A programme I worked very hard to be part of. Backing out now would virtually get me blacklisted from every other programme that exists.' Panic gripped his chest.

The lawyer seemed nonplussed. 'I'm sure other staff

have family situations that have to be dealt with. If you let them know what's happened, I think you'll find they will be quite understanding. And there will be other residencies—other surgical programmes.'

'Spoken like a true lawyer with no understanding of the medical profession and just how competitive things actually are,' Duc snapped.

Quang acted as though he hadn't heard. He pushed a few pieces of paper towards Duc and held a pen towards him. 'I need your signature on a few items.'

Duc stiffened. Hostility sweeping through him. A hand came over and squeezed his knee. He glanced sideways. He could see the tension in the muscles at the bottom of Viv's neck. She was trying very, very hard to stay quiet right now. 'What if I refuse?'

Quang's eyebrow moved a few millimetres upwards. 'Your staff won't get paid. Deliveries of supplies to the hospital will cease, and there will be no budget to pay for all the tests you send to the labs.'

He had him. Of course he did.

Duc snatched the pen from his hand and scribbled his signature on the three pieces of paper. The air in the office was stifling. He had to get out of there. He walked out without another word and strode back down the stairs. He could hear Vivienne's light footsteps running behind him.

But as he burst out into the bright sunlight, he knew immediately the error of his ways. The heat outside was every bit as warm as in the office. He couldn't seem to catch a cool breath.

'Duc!' Vivienne's voice was loud behind him and she clamped down her hand on his arm. 'What on earth just happened in there?'

The heat was starting to get to her hair. It was getting a little frizzy around the edges. And, from the look of Vivienne, she was getting a little frizzy around the edges too. Her mouth was set in a harsh line.

'My career just divebombed out the window,' he replied. He glanced around them. 'Come with me.' He grabbed hold of her hand and led her across the street to a franchise of a popular coffee chain. The air-conditioning blasted them as soon as they walked through the door. It only took a few moments to order some coffee and cake and take a seat in one of the booths.

Duc could feel the sweat that had emerged on his skin instantly cooling. He undid the button on his collar and pulled his tie down. Viv undid the button on her collar too. Her thin gold chain was nestled against her skin.

Before he could think, his fingers had reached across the table. 'You still wear that?'

On anyone else, this would be an intrusive move, but with Viv it felt entirely natural. His fingers rested on the chain and gave it a little tug upwards, revealing the gold butterfly with pale blue tourmaline stones in its wings.

Her hand came up and caught the pendant. 'Of course I still wear it,' she said sharply.

He'd bought it for her a few years ago for her birthday. It had been an entirely spur-of-the-moment purchase. He'd been walking through a shopping arcade in one of the more prestigious parts of Chicago when it had caught his eye in a window display.

Viv had joked the year before that no man had ever bought her jewellery, but as soon as he'd seen the pale blue in the butterfly's wings it had reminded him of the blue of her eyes. He'd bought and shipped it that day. It had gone clean out of his head until this very second.

He dropped his hand and gave her a smile. 'You told me no man had ever bought you jewellery.'

She stared at him for a few seconds. He was well aware of the fact he was avoiding the elephant in the room, and he didn't doubt for a second that Viv knew it too.

She leaned her head on one hand and dropped the pendant, letting it dangle between the curves of her breasts outlined by her shirt. She lifted her spoon and stirred her cappuccino round and round.

'No man has.' Her lips quipped upwards.

He didn't take the bait. Just stared at the random cakes he'd just bought sitting on the plates in front of them.

Her fingers drummed on the table. 'I guess this wasn't exactly what you expected,' she said softly.

'Nope.' The anger was still thrumming through his body. He'd loved his parents dearly, but he'd never expressed any interest in taking over from them at the community hospitals. They'd always known his plan was to be a surgeon. Why on earth would they not have made better plans?

His hands clenched into fists. 'This is a mess. A complete and utter mess. I shouldn't be here. I shouldn't be doing *this*.' The last word was said through gritted teeth.

Silence encompassed them.

Viv wasn't normally the type to keep quiet. Whilst she always had a good manner with patients, Duc had seen her stand up to arrogant colleagues, wipe the floor with rude medical students, and question incompetent methods at every turn. One question. That was all she'd asked. He glanced at his watch. They'd been in here more than ten minutes. The fact she'd been this quiet this long wasn't a good sign.

'Spit it out, Viv. I feel like I'm dangling from the cliff edge already. Just spit it out.'

Her shoulders went down, and her chin tilted up. He still couldn't get away from the businesswoman look she was sporting today. He'd always known Viv wasn't someone to mess with, but today, with the smart skirt, shirt and heels, she looked like she was about to wipe out a whole boardroom.

Or him, at the very least.

She clasped her hands on the table and looked him straight in the eye. 'I love you, Duc, but it's time to get a grip on things.'

The words hit him like a punch to the stomach. He opened his mouth to object, but this new ultra-calm incarnation of Vivienne wasn't finished with him yet.

'What happened to your mum and dad is awful. Absolutely awful. I admired them, and I know you did too. But they've left behind something that matters, Duc. That really *matters* and if you don't get a grip, you're going to ruin everything.'

He knew that. Of course he knew that. But he couldn't help how he felt deep down inside. He let out a huge sigh. 'But this was their dream, Viv. Not mine.' Even the words felt weary.

She shot him a look of impatience. 'It wasn't just their dream. This is their *legacy*, Duc. They've done so much good—not just at May Mắn Hospital, but at the other two hospitals as well. Think of all the patients who wouldn't have had treatment. Diseases picked up, infections prevented by immunisations. Can you imagine what would have happened to all those people if your mum and dad hadn't dreamed big?'

She was doing the big-picture stuff. The stuff that

made him realise how selfish he was being right now. But was it really selfish to work your guts out for ten years to become a surgeon, only to have it whipped away because of a terrible accident and a pile of legalities?

She took another breath and gave her head a small shake. 'You don't have the same drive and passion for the hospital that they had. That Lien has. Maybe that's just because you've never seen it in your plans or your future, but...' she took a breath '...plans change. People have to adjust their plans all the time, and now it's time to adjust yours.'

This was her no-argument voice. He'd heard it before.

'May Mắn Hospital is an essential part of the community. Starting tomorrow, things are changing. This afternoon we draw up adverts for another midwife, an obstetrician, and for some admin support. You need someone to keep on top of the paperwork for you.' She put her hand to her chest. '*I* need some assurance that staff are working safely. I'm going to download all the procedures and protocols from the last place I worked. We'll adapt them.' She looked him right in the eye. 'Together. This is your inheritance, Duc. Your responsibility.'

She was right. He knew she was right. She reached over and grabbed a bit of cake from under his nose and took a bite.

He spoke quietly. 'They inspire me, Viv. Just like they inspire everyone who works with them.' He grimaced, realising he was still using present tense for his parents. He couldn't help it.

He kept going. 'It's a lot to live up to. What if I'm not as good as them? What if this really isn't the job for me? I guess—at the back of my mind—I always thought that if I did come back here, I'd be a fully qualified surgeon. I'd have fulfilled my career ambitions. I'd come back here with a whole lot more experience than I currently have. You said yourself—between them—look at the host of things they covered. Not many doctors have the skill set to do that. Medical issues, infectious diseases, surgery, obstetrics, paediatrics. These are all specialist fields.'

He took a deep breath. 'People who come to work here have heard the reputation. They expect to be inspired by the Nguyens.' He put his hand on his chest. 'What if they don't get that from me?'

She stared out of the window. Her voice was a little wistful, with a tang of slight envy. 'You don't get it. You have something. You really have something. Something that can make a difference. Do you know what I inherited from my parents? Probably cancer genes from one and an addictive personality from the other.'

Another punch to the stomach. He got it. He did.

He'd had a family. He'd had years of love and support from his parents. Viv had never experienced anything like that. No wonder she was calling him out.

He hung his head, watching his career in surgery waving goodbye for the time being.

Her voice cut into his thoughts again. Her hand brushed against his. 'And why won't people be inspired by you, Duc? I am. Always have been.' She let the words hang between them for a few seconds. He didn't really even have time to process them before she started again. 'And you can't be miserable.'

'What?' Now he frowned.

She pointed a finger. 'You can't act as if this is the last place you want to be. You have to be positive. You have to try and get the staff to embrace the changes. If you walk around with a long face, either Lien will end up punching you or I will. This can only work if *you* make it work.' She spoke quietly. 'The staff need you right now—not just the patients. They're bereaved too. Your mum and dad were reliable and loyal to their staff. They knew everything about them. You need to fill that gap.'

Nothing like piling on the pressure. But in a way he needed this. Only Viv knew when he needed a kick up the backside, and she was exactly the person to do it. And it wasn't just that. It was the fire and determination in her eyes as she said it. It sent endorphins flooding through his system in the weirdest possible way. Was this the way Viv looked in the bedroom?

Where had that thought come from? He gave himself a shake. If it were possible, he'd just shocked even himself.

It was almost like he could feel a gentle smoke settle around him, resting on his shoulders and making him try and clear his thoughts.

Behaving like a kid and shouting, 'This isn't fair!' in between grieving for his parents wouldn't do any good at all. Mixing it up with weird thoughts about Viv made it even more confusing.

He had to get his head back into the game. He pulled his eyes away from that pendant dangling down her neck and resting on her curves.

He would ask for a temporary suspension from the surgical programme. He would have a meeting with all the staff at the hospital to tell them they all had to try and work together to do business as usual.

He'd get to the job adverts. He'd let Viv take the lead on the midwifery protocols. His head was already forming a list of admin tasks for the new assistant, not least finding some computer software that could help with the rota systems of three separate hospitals.

Viv's blue eyes met his. He was ready for a whole new onslaught but she seemed to realise that in this case less was more. She pushed the remaining doughnut towards him. 'Eat up.' She gave him an easy smile. 'Somehow I think you're going to need it.'

CHAPTER SIX

FOR THE FIRST week she wondered if she'd been too harsh. As she replayed the shock on Duc's face in the lawyer's office, and then again once they'd got outside, she wondered if she'd almost crossed the line into being a little mean.

Part of her got it. He was literally watching his career dreams slip through his fingers like grains of sand on the beach. He hadn't been joking when he'd told the lawyer that the competition for positions was tough. He'd now requested a temporary suspension. Who knew if the hospital board would look on his request kindly or not?

Viv had downloaded a whole heap of maternity protocols and Mai Ahn, the translator, had helped her translate them into Vietnamese. She now had folders with protocols in both languages, with the most important laminated and put up in the non-clinical areas as visual reminders.

The job adverts had been written and placed. The schedule had been juggled amongst the existing doctors. The antenatal clinics were busy. There were a few patients giving them cause for concern, and Vivienne had arranged a few case conference calls with an obstetrician in the main city hospital to get some professional expertise and to put plans in place.

Whilst there was a first flurry of activity, she quickly learned that within May Mắn hospital it paid to be adaptable.

The antenatal clinics only ran two days a week. The rest of the time, if there wasn't a woman currently in labour, she had a little time on her hands. Yes, she could put plans in place for different ways of doing things, service enhancements and a review of all equipment, but most of all Viv was conscious of how much she was currently treading water.

The staff was still getting used to Khiem and Hoa not being around. Every now and then someone would mention them as if they were still there, or Viv would catch a wistful look from a staff member lost in their own thoughts.

It wouldn't do to try and change too much at once. Not until she'd really had a chance to see what was best for the staff and patients around here. She'd experienced many areas where a new staff member or manager had charged in, full of enthusiastic plans, without taking stock of where they were, or the population they served. Just because something worked wonderfully well in a city landscape, it didn't mean it would work well in a rural one. She'd seen too many past disasters to create one of her own.

So Viv had learned to be a willing pair of hands. She dressed wounds, helped with some of the elderly patients, assisted with patient procedures, and even helped out in Theatre when Reuben, the plastic surgeon, visited. She hadn't quite got to the bottom of what the story was about him. But as soon as he'd heard her accent he'd queried if she was a relative of Joe's. She'd met his question with amusement. 'Scotland's a pretty big place. There is more than one family.' He'd kept his questions to a minimum after that.

She liked helping out. Although her first love was midwifery, she enjoyed using her nursing skills elsewhere when it was appropriate and it also helped her get to know all the staff a little better. She still had some challenges with the language, but she was trying hard, and the patients and staff seemed to appreciate it.

There was something about this place. She normally adapted well to new places. But Hanoi just felt different. A more vibrant community. A more international place. She was quickly learning the places to shop, the street markets to go to and the best places to eat.

She'd even picked up Lien and Joe's son a few times from nursery when they'd both been busy at work. Regan was a cute little guy. Whenever she was with him, it was like both their Scottish accents got stronger and stronger. By the time they'd walked the street back to the hospital only Joe could understand them both.

But she liked it. The staff here welcomed her, included her in things. She'd been for drinks to celebrate a secret wedding, a thirtieth birthday party and a buffet party at someone's house. It was nice to feel included. With the exception of being around Duc, it had been a long time since she'd felt like that.

She turned the corner to the offices and saw Duc sitting behind his father's desk. Even she still thought of it as Khiem's, so how must he feel?

She stopped in the doorway and folded her arms. 'Hey,' she said softly.

He looked up, his eyes tired. 'Hey, yourself.' He

pushed away the laptop in front of him. 'How many did you deliver today?'

She smiled. 'Just the one. And she was very obliging and perfect in every way.'

She crossed the room and stood next to him. 'When was the last time you ate?'

He didn't really meet her gaze. For the last few weeks they'd been like ships passing in the night, both of them so busy that there hadn't been time to sit down together, let alone to eat.

She cracked a smile. 'I don't know, you invite a girl here, get her to work, cover all the shifts, and you can't even buy her dinner?'

He met her gaze. He knew she was teasing him. She gave him a nudge. 'Come on, Mr Cool. Lien and Joe are covering tonight. Joe might have suggested we get out of here for a bit.'

'He did?'

She nodded. 'I think they worry. Come on, there must be somewhere good around here you can take me. Can't remember the last time I had a good dinner.'

For the briefest second she thought he might try and make some kind of excuse. But he shook his head and stood up, lifting his jacket from the back of the chair. 'Tell me what you want to eat.'

She closed her eyes for a second, imagining her dream dinner. 'Fish. Sea bass if it's available anywhere around here.'

He looked at her burgundy scrubs. 'I know just the place, but you'd better get changed.'

She wrinkled her nose and stretched out the leg of her scrubs. 'What, you don't like the colour?'

He shook his head. 'Come on.' He glanced at his

watch. 'I'll call and make us a reservation. Can you be ready in half an hour?'

'Race you.' There was a glint in her eye. He wanted to laugh out loud. Whenever they'd worked together it had been a standing joke that you didn't want to be in Viv's way when she was racing to the hospital canteen. It seemed that nothing had changed. He smiled. There was something about the familiarity that spread a warm feeling throughout him. Viv was the last real person he had a connection to—a connection that felt as if it counted. As he turned to close the door to the office the paperwork on the desk caught his eye.

Out of nowhere a thought shot into his head. Routine hospital paperwork included the patient giving their next of kin. His skin prickled. He'd only had a few hospital admissions his entire life. A few stitches as a kid. A broken wrist. It didn't matter that he'd been an adult for years and had never needed to name a next of kin. But if he needed to, who would he name now?

Vivienne. Her name washed through him. Now his next of kin would be Vivienne. There was no one else. As he pulled the door closed another thought crossed his mind—one he'd never considered before. For as long as he'd known her, Vivienne had had no close relations. So who did she name?

She stepped out of the bedroom after pulling the sides of her hair back with a delicate clasp that Lien had loaned her.

Duc made a noise just to her left. She spun around and looked down. 'What? Is there a mark on it?'

He had a strange expression on his face. She'd grabbed one of the few nicer pieces in her wardrobe.

She'd only ever worn it once before. A red knee-length, off-the-shoulder fitted dress. It hugged her curves, the thick red lace bonded over a perfectly matched lining.

She slid her feet into her heels. The only jewellery she was wearing was her butterfly pendant. Her fingers went to her neck. She knew it didn't really match, but she didn't like to take it off.

Duc was still staring at her. He'd changed into dark trousers, a white shirt and a matching dark jacket. 'What's this?' she joked. 'The James Bond look?'

His eyes were wide. She'd moved over right next to him. She glanced down again self-consciously. 'What is it?' She twisted from side to side, trying to see if there was a split in one of her side seams.

It was almost as if Duc had been in a trance. He blinked and shook his head, a smile dancing at the edges of his lips. 'I've never really seen you in real party gear. It suits you. You should wear it more often. Just like the business look the other day—you almost scared me.'

She lifted her eyebrows. 'The business look? Duc, those are my interview clothes.' She gave a half-shrug, then a little nod of her head. 'To be honest, they've been pretty lucky. I've got every job I've ever gone for in that outfit.'

He laughed. 'You'd get every job in that red dress too. Where have you been hiding that?'

She ran her hands across her stomach, smoothing down the fabric. 'I saw it in a shop window, walked in and bought it. I never even tried it on—to be honest, I'm lucky that it fitted.' She gave a sigh. 'I bought it out of spite really.'

'Spite?' Now he was intrigued. 'What do you mean?'

She held up one hand to her hair. 'I'm a redhead, you

might have noticed, and I spent my entire childhood with people telling me I couldn't wear red—no matter how much I liked the colour—that it just didn't suit me. So, I saw the dress, had just been paid, and decided I was buying it.'

He gave her a soft smile. 'Well, from where I'm standing, it was a good decision. A great decision.' He lifted a hand a tugged a little strand of her hair forward. 'Your hair's a dark red, it's dramatic. It suits it perfectly.'

She looked up into his dark eyes. Duc didn't normally give her compliments—they were more the type of friends to constantly spar with each other. This felt... different. For the first time she wasn't quite sure what to say.

He tilted his elbow out towards her. 'Shall we?'

She grinned. 'I'd love to.'

As they reached the door, he grabbed her coat. 'Did you put on your mosquito repellent?'

She rolled her eyes at him. 'Of course I did.'

He gave a nod. 'Still, better cover up. Your dress is gorgeous, but for the mosquitos you show too much skin.'

She sighed and slipped her hands into the coat, fastening it up to the neck. 'By the time we reach the restaurant I will be a humid mess.'

He shook his head. 'Don't worry, it's not far.'

They walked across the grass, through the hospital, and out into the main street.

There was something nice about getting away from the hospital. They'd rarely left the premises together since they'd got here.

Duc pointed out some of the local places to Viv. 'It's been five years since you were last here. This is the place the food cart stops during the day. It has the best noodle soups, like *hủ tiếu*—the pork base with noodles—and *bún riêu*—the crab and tomato broth—which are the nicest. Then there's *bánh mì*, with freshly baked baguettes that just melt in your mouth. But remember, most street food vendors here change their menu every day. Try and make it when the *chả giò*—the crispy spring rolls—are on.'

Vivienne was rapidly trying to store all the words in her brain. 'You know I have been walking around here, finding my own favourite places.'

'You have?' He looked surprised.

'Of course I have.' She laughed. 'I'm a big girl. I get out and about. I've lived in ten different cities. I've learned to find the best food.' She laughed again. 'You know food's my priority. It's almost like I have an in-built antenna. But I might need to make a few notes in my phone.'

Duc gave her an appreciative stare, as if he hadn't quite realised she had been finding her own feet. He pointed at a building across the street with bright blue shutters. 'And that's the shop where they sell those candies that you like.'

Her footsteps faltered. 'You remember that?'

He rolled his eyes. 'How can I forget? I had to keep asking my mum to ship me some so I could send them to you.'

A wave of sadness flashed across his eyes at the memory and she tugged him a little closer without saying anything. She didn't need to. She just looked around her. 'I'd forgotten how much I love this place,' she sighed.

He looked surprised. 'You do?'

She nodded slowly as they strolled down the brightly

lit street. 'Look at the buildings up ahead.' She pointed to the row of shops with red, blue and yellow awnings. Packed above and looking kind of squished together was a multitude of flats—all entirely individual. There was one column in pink brick with a balcony on each level, the next column was white, with plants trailing down to the awning beneath, then came the thinnest column of flats that Viv had ever seen. One had a balcony packed with a dining table and chairs. The one above was crowded with a whole array of children's toys. The one nearest the top had given over the entire balcony to green foliage, with dashes of brightly coloured flowers.

Viv smiled and hugged Duc's arm. 'This place is just packed with character. That's what I love about it. Where else would you see such a great array of colours?' She took a deep breath. 'And smell such a fabulous aroma of food.' Her eyes were gleaming. 'This place had better be close, or you're gonna get crazy low blood sugar, Viv, and we both know that isn't good.'

He laughed and led her to a black door in one of the side streets, revealing a glass-fronted elegant-looking restaurant.

Viv frowned and did a double-take. 'Is this place a secret? It looks a little out of place.'

He tapped the side of his nose. 'It's a closely guarded secret. The food in here is brilliant. You asked for sea bass and you won't find better.'

He opened the door and they were greeted by a head waiter who took Viv's jacket and led them to a pristine table, covered in a white linen tablecloth. He took their drinks order then left them with menus and Viv leaned across the table towards Duc. 'Uh-oh, I look at a tablecloth like this and want to take bets on how long it will take me to spill something on it.'

He shook his head. 'Well, you look the part, now you just have to act the part.'

Her eyes widened in mock horror. 'How dare you?'

He shrugged. 'It's payback. You told me to man up a few weeks ago.'

She smiled. This was them. This was the way they always had been, and she instantly felt relaxed again. The last few weeks had been...odd.

She knew Duc was under enormous strain, but there had something weird in the air between them too. Something she couldn't quite put her finger on. It was moments like this that made her realise just how deep their friendship was cemented and that filled her with relief.

The waiter arrived with their drinks then took their order. Viv glanced around. The restaurant was busy, but it wasn't noisy. There was kind of a quiet ambience, people spoke and laughed quietly, giving the place an intimacy that wasn't apparent from the glass frontage. It was clear just from looking around that the clientele were wealthy. Hanoi was a real mixed bag, with pockets of real wealth and real poverty, and Viv wondered if she really fitted in here.

She lifted her glass of wine to Duc. 'Let's have a toast.'

He nodded and picked up his glass too. 'What are we drinking to?'

She grinned. 'Well, last time around we were in a beach bar, with bottles of—quite possibly—the worst beer we'd ever tasted.' She blinked and pressed her lips together. 'I think we toasted new beginnings then.'

He sucked in a breath. He'd been due to start at the

Philadelphia hospital, and she'd just got a new job in London at that point. They'd met for a crazy week in Ibiza, which was blurry around the edges.

She gave a sigh. 'I think I spent most of that week in those denim shorts.'

He rolled his eyes. 'Or that black bikini. Did it finally die a death due to overuse?'

She laughed again. 'It went where all my clothes go to die—the tumble dryer!'

He held up his wine and mimicked her Scottish accent. 'If it cannae go in the tumble dryer there's no point havin' it!'

She was still holding her glass up. 'Is that going to be our toast?'

He shook his head, the laughter leaving his eyes. 'No. I guess we should stick to the original. New beginnings. It seems kind of apt, in an entirely different way.'

She swallowed and nodded her head. He looked serious now for the first time since they'd got in here. She wished she could take away the black cloud that seemed to have settled around Duc's shoulders from the first instant she'd arrived. She'd wanted to steal back a moment of the old Duc. The one who made her laugh until her sides ached. Who was happy to stay up until three in the morning discussing the latest sci-fi series and where it had all gone wrong.

Would she ever get that back? Her insides ached at the thought. Bereavement changed people. Of course it did. She knew that. She'd never been the same girl after her own adoptive parents had died. But witnessing her best friend being so out of his depth was hard. Duc had always been capable and more than competent. Ambitious and dedicated, with an edge of fun. Right now, only glimmers of the real Duc were shining through. She knew he was there. She just had to try and bring him back.

She lifted her glass and clinked it against his. 'To new beginnings. For both of us.'

His smile didn't quite reach his eyes as he lifted his glass to his lips.

The waiter appeared and sat down their plates in front of them. Sea bass with sizzled ginger, chilli and spring onions on a bed of noodles for Viv, and Vietnamese marinated flank steak for Duc. He closed his eyes for a few seconds while he was eating and let out a moan. 'Mmm… I'd forgotten just how good this place was.'

'You come here a lot?' The sea bass was delicious, tasting just as good as its succulent aroma.

He nodded. 'Every time I've been back.' He never added anything else and a wave of something washed over her.

'With your mum and dad?'

He gave a slow nod. She could see that memories were filling his head. He gave a visible shake and picked up his glass again. 'And with friends, sometimes visiting doctors, trying to tempt them to stay.'

Viv looked around with a smile. 'Ah, so this is the charm machine.'

'The what?' He looked amused.

She held out her hands. 'The place where you do all your schmoozing.' She looked around again with an appreciative nod then frowned and looked back at him. 'Should I be offended this is the first time you've brought me? I've visited you here more than once.'

Duc pulled a face, realising he was in trouble. 'I've

never needed to schmooze you before. Because…' he paused for a second '…you're Viv.'

She took another bite of her fish. 'I'm not sure whether to be offended or complimented.'

She held her cutlery at either side of her plate. 'I feel cheated. Others have been wined and dined. I've been bought the occasional beer.'

'Uh-oh. Are you about to renegotiate your contract?'

'You need to give me one first,' she quipped. 'And this fish…' she pointed her fork down at the plate '…has to be a compulsory part of it. A restaurant visit on a weekly basis will have to be part of my contract.' She raised one eyebrow, pausing for a second as their gazes connected. 'If you still want me to stay, that is.'

She wasn't quite sure where it had come from. Or why she would say it now. But she'd dropped everything to be here for Duc. And the truth was she had no real job security. No guarantee. She'd learned early on in life to be self-sufficient. For Viv, that always meant dotting the i's and crossing the t's. Every lease was double-checked. Contracts were in her hand before she gave notice at the last job. Insurance was always in place. She'd more or less thrown all that out of the window to be here for Duc.

But something else was unsettling her. It had been since she'd got here—but she hadn't quite been able to put her finger on it. They'd always been so easy around each other. So comfortable. She'd put the strange feeling down to Duc being upset at losing his parents. But the more she was around him, she realised it wasn't just him. It was her too. Things just felt different between them. And the truth was it scared her. Running away was what she did best—but she'd never run from Duc before.

Duc froze. 'Of course I want you to stay. Why would you say that?'

She lowered her gaze and started pushing her food around the plate. 'I don't know. You've seen the lawyer now. You know what lies ahead. We've made some plans. Maybe you think you can take things forward yourself?'

He put his cutlery down and leaned towards her. 'Are you crazy? Why on earth do you think I don't need you? I need you more than ever.'

She gave a slow nod. Some reassurance swept through her, along with an unexpected squeeze of her heart. Everything just felt so unsettled right now.

His gaze narrowed but his voice was laced with anxiety. 'You've only been here a few weeks. You can't be ready to move on already. You just told me that you love this place.'

She bit her lip. 'I do. But you know me, I never stay anywhere for long.'

'Most places you give at least six months.' He wrinkled his nose. 'The other place—the one you were working at. Do they expect you back?' The worry on his face was evident.

She almost choked on her fish. 'Are you kidding? I think I've burnt my bridges there. Leaving without giving proper notice?'

He rested his hands on the table. 'Then why are you in such a hurry to leave here, to leave me?'

The words wouldn't really form in her brain. She couldn't really explain where the question had come from. It had just happened like that. Sometimes she was at a place, and just got an overwhelming sensation that it might be time to move on. Granted, it never usually took just a few weeks, but all her of senses felt out of alignment right now—and she couldn't fathom why.

She let out a long slow breath. 'Oh, you know me. I always have a wobble.'

'Is it me?' His dark eyes were staring right at her, sucking her in. Making her feel completely self-conscious. He ran his fingers through his hair. 'Darn it. I'm not myself right now. I know I'm not.'

Maybe she was going crazy. Maybe this was all her in head. But her automatic reaction to feelings she couldn't explain was to run in the opposite direction. *That* was where the question had come from.

Because the thought of staying here, with Duc, for any longer was doing strange things to her mind.

'Stay, give me the six months that you normally give everywhere else. By then, plans should be in place. There should be some new, permanent staff. I can't do this without you. You know I can't.'

His hand reached across the table and his fingers intertwined with hers. A jolt of heat shot up her arm. Maybe it was the wine. She was on her second glass. But for some reason she didn't want to let go.

'Six months,' she said softly. 'Six months and then we both go back to where we belong?'

Her stomach was clenched, because even as she said the words she wasn't sure if she could do it.

And she didn't want to make promises she couldn't keep.

Especially to Duc.

But his smile broadened and he gave a nod. 'Six months. We'll have it all worked out by then. I promise you.'

She hesitantly lifted her glass and clinked it against the one he offered while her stomach tumbled over and over.

Because for the first time another thought entered her head. Was six months really enough? Or would it turn out to be too long?

Maybe she wasn't the only one making promises she couldn't keep...

CHAPTER SEVEN

HE WAS FINALLY starting to get to grips with things. The new administrator was fabulous. Sen had worked as a PA at a Fortune 500 company and decided to take early retirement. Working for a place like May Mắn Hospital was exactly what she wanted. She'd sat across the desk from Duc at her interview and, after five minutes, had sighed and written him a list of all the things he needed to get in order. She'd started work after he'd taken her for coffee and cake across the road.

For the first time since he'd got here it felt like a little part of the weight was off his shoulders. Sen regularly had a stacked pile on his desk awaiting signature, then would wave him off with her favourite comment. 'Go, be a doctor!'

Today he was covering partly in one of the drop-in clinics and partly on the wards.

One of the nurses called him in to assess a man with a leg ulcer. Lots of older patients had poor circulation, which caused slow healing of any injuries. Duc checked the man's notes. This leg ulcer had been there for more than eight months. Whilst some ulcers never healed, with correct treatment most could heal in three to four months.

He peeled back the bandages, taking care not to damage any of the surrounding skin. The ulcer was smothered in a thick gel and covered with a non-adherent dressing. As soon as he started cleaning it, he noticed a slight discharge and a strange aroma. He asked a few questions, then leaned back.

He walked over to the cupboards and came back with some new products. Viv appeared at his side. 'What are you doing?'

'Leg ulcer.'

Her nose wrinkled. 'Okay, new skill. It's time to learn.'

He gave her a smile. 'What, midwives don't deal with leg ulcers?'

'Debrided wounds, yes. Leg ulcers? No. Thankfully, most of my patients are in a slightly younger age range. But in the future, who knows?'

Duc nodded as he picked up a wound swab and sterile bag. 'Well, it's one of the common things you'll see in the outpatient clinics. Might as well get used to them.'

She moved over and introduced herself to the patient in stilted Vietnamese. She was getting better. He was impressed.

Duc acted as translator as he swabbed the wound. He'd already decided to prescribe some antibiotics. 'Look at the edges of the wound, there's some redness and swelling, add in the discharge and slight odour and...' He let his voice tail off.

'You have an infection,' replied Vivienne. She moved a little closer to study the edges and depth of the ulcer.

Duc nodded. 'I think it's likely. A lot of venous ulcers that don't heal have an underlying bacterial infection.'

Viv shot him a curious glance as she looked at the

dressings on the sterile tray. 'So, do you put the same thing back on, or do you try something else?'

He waggled his hand. 'Actually, a bit of both. We'll keep using the alginate gel. There's lots of good research on its effectiveness. But I'm also going to add in a silver-based wound dressing that helps combat infections.'

Vivienne gave a smile. 'A two-pronged attack.'

Duc nodded as he spoke to the patient and finished dressing the wound. 'Let's make it a three-pronged attack. Compression bandage to finish to help keep swelling down. This has gone on long enough.'

Vivienne automatically stood to help with the tidying up as Lien appeared at the door. 'Oh, good, you're both here. Can I grab you once you're finished?'

Duc gave the patient the antibiotics, along with some instructions and a return appointment. He followed Viv into the next room where Lien was standing with her arms folded.

'What's wrong? You look worried.'

Lien nodded. 'I am. You know that Joe gets these ideas in his head.'

Vivienne's brow creased and Duc realised she'd no idea what they were talking about.

He put his hand on Viv's shoulder. 'Joe's from your neck of the woods. He likes to try and do home visits. Set up more community clinics.'

'Is that bad?' Viv held up her hands. 'That's just normal.'

Lien shot her a look. 'I have a hard enough time getting my husband to toe the line. Don't you encourage him.'

'What's the problem, then?' Viv had mirrored Lien's position and folded her arms across her chest. It was almost like they were in direct competition with each other.

Lien turned her attention to Duc. 'We've had a few patients with unusual symptoms and Joe decided to investigate.' She looked sideways at Viv. 'Two of the women are pregnant.'

Viv instantly straightened. 'Where are they?'

Lien pressed her lips together. 'Everyone in the family is sick. They all stay in a building a few streets away. At a guess, there are eight family members. Two elderly parents, a son and daughter who are both married with a child of their own.'

'They can't get in to the clinic?' Duc asked—even though he could already guess the answer.

Lien shook her head. 'All of them have fevers, muscle and joint pain—so severe they can hardly get of bed. Throw in some nausea, vomiting and other GI symptoms.'

Duc let out a long slow breath. 'It could virtually be anything from norovirus to dengue fever, zika or chikungunya. Even food poisoning, or a weird strain of malaria.'

He nodded slowly. 'Okay, Lien, you know I've been working in Surgical lately. But I still remember all the basics.' He turned to Viv. 'I'll need to brief you on a few of these as they might not be too familiar.' He nodded again, decision made. 'Lien, call Joe. Tell him that we'll join him at the address in around an hour. Are you okay to cover the hospital?'

She nodded and he paused for a second. 'Lien, can you organise some supplies to take with us, and I'll brief Viv and arrange some transport for us.'

Lien's tight shoulders dropped, as if some of the tension had just left her body. It was clear she was relieved that Joe wasn't going to be left in that situation alone.

Duc hurried down the corridor with Viv close behind him. 'I'm going to give you some crib sheets.'

'What?'

He smiled and reached for a folder above the desk. 'Sen found a whole pile of things randomly filed by my dad. It seemed he made crib sheets for some of the international doctors on conditions that crop up in Vietnam that aren't so well known in other countries. Just to give them some first line information. She's duplicated and filed them all in here.' He raised his eyebrows. 'Apparently, in future we're going to have induction packs for staff. Maybe even send the information beforehand to let them study it.'

Viv looked around the office and smiled. 'This place looks a whole lot tidier.'

Duc paused and gave a thoughtful nod. 'It is. My parents loved being doctors too much to worry about the paperwork. Sen has been a blessing. She's gone through this place with military precision. I think half the contents ended up shredded because they were out of date or not important any more. She's scanned some things for electronic filing and cleared out the filing cabinets and reorganised the rest.' He gestured to the seat behind the desk. 'I can actually pull the chair in now, instead of having to dodge the boxes under the desk.'

He pulled out the sheets for Viv. 'And watch out. She's got her eye on how we deal with patient records. Apparently, she's also getting us a quote about electronic prescribing.'

Viv nodded as she stared down at the crib sheets.

For the first time since she'd got here she looked a little swamped.

Duc put his hand on her shoulder. 'Don't worry. Lien and I will talk you through anything.'

Viv shook her head. 'Zika. I heard news reports about it, but I just never had a patient who'd been exposed.' She pulled a face. 'So I didn't really read up on it. Now I'm feeling like a prize idiot.'

Duc squeezed her shoulder. 'You're never an idiot. This is an entirely new place. Look at what you did a couple of hours after you arrived.' His face grew serious. 'And you have no idea how relieved I am that you were here.'

He waited for a few seconds, giving her time to get over the little burst of nerves. 'Now, let me talk to Sen and organise the transport. Sit down for ten minutes and give yourself the chance to read the basics. I'll shout for you when we're ready to go.'

Duc walked back down the corridor, giving some instructions to Sen and then pulling his phone out of his pocket and calling Joe's number. 'Hello, crazy Scot number two, tell me what you've got.'

It was the first time since she'd got here that she felt nervous about her clinical skills. She'd always known that there were diseases endemic to Vietnam, and if this had been a job she'd applied for, she would have researched them completely. But there hadn't been time, and she'd just been so caught up in getting to Duc that she hadn't really thought about the job properly.

Her first experience had thrown her in at the deep end. She'd quickly taken stock of the fact there was no functioning obstetrician and had taken steps to try and put safety measures in place.

But all her running around and organising had left her at a disadvantage. How could she really serve as an efficient and competent midwife or nurse if she didn't know the basics about the population? She was letting them down, and she was letting the hospital down. A single bead of sweat trailed down her back and she shifted uncomfortably. It was unbearably hot today.

She tried to memorise everything on the sheets—then pulled out her phone to search for specific effects on pregnant women. The conversation between Duc and Lien seemed accurate. At first glance, any of these conditions could be mistaken for each other—but all had different results. It was important to diagnose correctly.

Lien appeared at the door. 'Are you ready?' she asked.

Viv nodded and stood, but Lien pointed at the table. 'Put on some more mosquito repellent before we go.' She handed Viv a lightweight long-sleeved jacket. 'Just to be safe,' she added.

The journey only took ten minutes. Duc, Viv and Mai Ahn were packed into a four-by-four with a pile of equipment.

Viv watched out the window as they turned into a street on the outskirts of Hanoi. The street was cluttered with bikes, mopeds and trash cans. A number of washing lines hung between the tightly packed buildings.

She climbed out the car and watched as Joe opened a door nearby and gave them all a wave.

His brow was creased as they approached. 'Eight people. Most dehydrated and likely requiring some IV fluids. One of them is elderly, two are pregnant and two are kids.'

'Then we'll deal with them first,' said Duc. 'What about the rest of them?'

Joe handed over a notebook where he'd scribbled some notes. 'Most of them are pyrexial. Some are also hypotensive.'

Duc looked around and split the patients between them all. Viv found herself with the two pregnant women. Mai Ahn stayed by her side.

Vivienne looked around. The house was clearly in disarray—but when every member of the household was sick, that was no surprise. During her variety of jobs as a midwife she'd often worked in people's homes both during delivery and post-delivery.

Her first woman was paler than could be reasonable and was lying in bed, her breathing shallow. Vivienne sat down at the bedside and introduced herself, asking her name and for permission to check the woman over.

'This is Mai-Lyn. She's twenty-four, and sixteen weeks pregnant.' Mai Ahn pulled a sympathetic face. 'She didn't realise she was sick at first. She thought maybe she just had late symptoms of early morning sickness. She'd been fine up until that point.'

It only took Vivienne five minutes to do some general checks. Mai-Lyn was very dehydrated. She had marks on her skin that looked like infected mosquito bites. Her blood pressure was low and her temperature high and a quick finger-prick blood test also revealed low blood sugar. Vivienne asked some pregnancy-related questions. Mai-Lyn had been having severe stomach cramps, but there had been no bleeding.

Vivienne pulled out her portable sonogram machine, and smeared some gel on Mai-Lyn's abdomen, breathing a sigh of relief when the rapid noise of a heartbeat could be heard.

Duc appeared at Viv's side. 'What have you got?'

'Are we moving these people to hospital or treating them here?'

He looked around and sighed. 'They could all do with hospitalisation, but there is still a chance this could be infectious. For now, we'll treat them here.'

Viv nodded and stood up. 'In that case I need to set up some IV fluids, including some dextrose. I also want to administer some antipyretic for her temperature. She needs fluids quickly in the first instance. I think she's got some infected mosquito bites. What the mosquitos might have carried?' She looked up into his dark eyes. 'I'll let you experts get to the bottom of that. It could be anyone of the three conditions you showed me earlier.'

Duc nodded. 'Let's treat the symptoms and put the pieces together once we know all the patients are stable.' He handed her some blood bottles. 'Get some samples when you set up the IV.'

Vivienne nodded and got to work, quickly taking the sample and then setting up an IV, then moved on to the other pregnant woman. Her symptoms were almost identical but her history of mosquito bites went back a few days earlier.

She treated her patient and made her way back through to Duc, who was conferring with Joe.

'I'm concerned by just how much joint pain both my ladies have. They've been bed bound for the last few days. One has a particularly nasty rash too. Is there anything safe to give them for the mosquito bites? A cream perhaps, as well as the antibiotics? I'm worried they'll end up breaking the skin they're both scratch-ing so much.'

Joe pulled out a medical bag and rummaged through it, pulling out a mild steroid cream. 'This should stop the itching and inflammation.' He gave her a look. 'If we were back home, I'd recommend a bath with por-ridge oats.'

She smiled. 'The well-known remedy for itchy chicken pox. I remember it well.' It was like a blast from the past. 'But, considering I wouldn't trust either of my pregnant women in a bath right now, I'll stick with the cream, thanks.'

She looked around the room. Most of the others had IVs running. She'd basically never seen such a dehy-drated bunch of patients in her life.

'This has hit really hard and fast,' she said. 'What on earth does this?'

'We're just deciding,' said Duc. 'It's crucial we get this right. Particularly for Zika—because that could have real implications for your pregnant women.'

Inside the pocket in her scrubs Vivienne secretly crossed her fingers. They still had to recruit another obstetrician. And if Zika was the diagnosis they needed one quickly.

Joe frowned. 'Most of the symptoms fitted with being unwell days after being bitten by mosquitos. The sudden fever, muscle and joint pains all fitted. Some have had headaches, fatigue and nausea. A few have GI symp-toms—and most have the nasty rash.'

Duc turned to him. 'You're thinking chikungunya?' He gave a considered nod.

Joe nodded. 'For me it's the joint pains being so in-tense and prolific. Other than that, the symptoms could literally be interchangeable.' He turned to Duc. 'What do you think?'

Duc was weighing everything up. 'It's just unusual. For some people chikungunya is symptomless,' he explained to Vivienne. 'But this has hit this family so hard and so fast it must be some kind of vicious strain.'

Viv wrinkled her nose. 'What does that mean? They've all been bitten by the same mosquito?'

Duc shook his head. 'No. One person usually gets bitten and becomes infectious. If they then get bitten by another mosquito, it can pass the virus to another person. Literally, the virus could have passed between them all in a matter of days.'

'Is there a cure? A treatment?' Viv asked hopefully. She hadn't got that far in the crib sheet yet—there just hadn't been time.

She liked the way they were discussing the case. They were all comparing notes, looking for the most likely cause.

Duc shook his head again. 'No cure. No vaccine. Just treatment. Those with underlying conditions, the young, and the elderly are most at risk of developing complications.'

'But if we keep our eye on this family over the next few days,' Joe said, 'by this time next week, they could all be on the road to recovery.'

Joe pulled some sample bottles from one of the bags. 'Okay, folks. Is there anyone we haven't taken blood from yet? We need to get samples and get them to the lab.'

Duc pointed to the two people who hadn't quite required IVs. 'Just these guys. I'll do it if you want.'

'I'm going to keep an eye on my ladies,' said Viv.

'One of them is having stomach cramps that I hope don't turn into anything else. I'm sure it's just a symptom of the disease but I'm going to keep an eye on her in case I need to recheck things.'

Joe pulled out some paperwork. 'Okay, let's get this up to date for each patient and make sure everything is charted and prescribed.' He raised his eyebrows. 'Then we'll have a chat about how we're going to manage this situation for the next few days.'

Viv put her hand up straight away. 'I'm happy to cover a few nights. I know I'm really a midwife, but general observations, IVs and antibiotics are all things I can cover—just as long as I'm not needed at the hospital.'

'How many patients do you have due right now?'

Viv pulled out the work phone that Sen had given to her that morning. 'Well, thanks to our wonder admin assistant I'll be able to tell you. Let me check. Yip. Twelve due this month. Seven have already delivered and we've had one from next month deliver already.' She gave them all a big smile. 'I actually don't have anyone due this week.'

Joe laughed. 'You know that means nothing. Let's hope you didn't just curse yourself by saying those words out loud.'

Vivienne laughed too. She liked how well everyone worked together. Teamwork was essential in any hospital, and the way that everyone had been willing to pack up and come out here had impressed her. Could they really have found ambulances to ferry all these people back to May Mắn? She simply wasn't sure.

She went back to check on her patients, turning up the speed on one of the IVs. Duc appeared and slung an arm around her shoulder. 'How do you feel about us both covering the night shift so we can send Joe home to his son?'

Viv nodded. 'Fine with me.'

Duc handed her a bottle of cream. 'First job for us to make sure everyone—including us—is covered from head to toe in mosquito repellent. There could still be virus-laden mosquitos hanging around. We don't want to be the next victims.'

Vivienne shuddered. 'You say the nicest things. Can I barter for another dinner for this?'

His eyes twinkled. 'I think I can manage another dinner.'

They worked comfortably together, settling down on the sofa in the main room once everyone had been tended to. Mai Ahn had come back with some extra bags of IV fluids and some food for them both.

It was dark outside now. Throughout the house they could hear the sounds of deep breathing. All the patients were sleeping.

Viv put her head on Duc's shoulder. 'I think I'm too tired to eat right now,' she murmured.

'You did good,' he said.

Her hand moved over to his arm. 'So did you. We all did. Let's just pray it's the right diagnosis.'

There was a long pause. Viv gazed at the dark sky speckled with stars outside the window.

'I'd forgotten about this part,' Duc said, his voice sounding a little strange.

She lifted her head. 'What?'

He made a sad kind of sound. 'The being a doctor and not just a surgeon part.' He held up one hand to gesture to the room they were sitting in. 'I would never do this, haven't done it in my whole career. I spend my life in a hospital setting, seeing patients in clinics, wards or Theatre.'

Viv smiled. 'Ah…a home visit virgin. Well, welcome to the world of community nursing. Every home opens a whole new world. You've no idea what you're stepping into.'

He looked at her and she continued. 'I've been in houses where they have giant birthing pools in their living rooms. Some where I've had to step over the passed-out drunk person as I step inside. Houses where my feet stick to the carpet and I'm afraid to take my coat off. Then there's the family pet who snarls and growls at me, looking as if they want to eat me, and there's the inevitable shout, "Don't worry, hen, he'll no' touch you!" Then…' she wagged her finger '…there's the pristine houses that are miles cleaner than the hospital and you feel positively shabby as soon as you cross the threshold.' She rolled her eyes. 'I've been asked to take my shoes off at the door or put those blue coveralls on my feet.'

He shook his head as he smiled back, his brown eyes looking at her fondly.

'Looking after people in their own environment is a privilege, Duc. I never forget that. And it makes you better at your job. You don't have a team to back you up. You can't press an emergency buzzer and a whole team appears in under two minutes. It's you. You're it. You have to improvise and make do. It makes a more experienced practitioner, and a more resilient one.'

He gave a slow nod of his head at her words. 'You love it, don't you?'

He pressed his lips together as she nodded. 'And I've taken you away from that.'

She squeezed his arm. 'There's lots of ways to look

after a community, Duc. According to Lien, she's practically had to put a tracker on Joe because he's so used to home visiting because he worked as a GP. Maybe there's a way to look at more outreach work. Or...' she held out her hand '...when it's needed, taking services to the patients. You did okay this time around.'

He leaned back against the sofa and Viv looked at the expression on his face. She saw something that hadn't been there before—curiosity.

'Every job can be a challenge. Sometimes the challenge is what gives you the enthusiasm to keep going.'

She wanted to say more. She wanted him to take a look around and realise just how important the work here was.

He'd risen to the challenge today. But his long-term plans weren't for working at May Mắn Hospital.

Her stomach gave a little twist. What were her own long-term plans? She'd never had any before. Just living from one six-month contract to the next.

But Hanoi was a wonderful city. Bright, exuberant and filled with special people. She could see a fantastic role here. One that she couldn't possibly even begin to tackle in six months.

She licked her lips, mouth suddenly dry. This was the first time ever she'd had thoughts like this. And what would be the point in thinking of staying here longer if Duc was going back to the US?

She leaned her head back on his shoulder and murmured, 'Okay, I bags first sleep. Wake me up in an hour.'

She settled down as he slung his arm around her shoulders again and let her snuggle against him. She'd think about all this later...

CHAPTER EIGHT

THE WEEKS PASSED QUICKLY. Vivienne started to become more familiar with the particular conditions that could affect the pregnant women around Hanoi.

Several of her patients had HIV and tuberculosis. They still didn't have a permanent obstetrician, but Joe had an interest in tuberculosis and helped her out with the complicated prescription regimes for her patients.

She was completing the paperwork for a new patient when Lien wandered into the treatment room.

'Hey.' She smiled as she started loading up a trolley for a chest drain.

'Hey. Oh, who needs a chest drain?'

'The tourist, Mr Hom. We've just done a chest X-ray.'

'Do you need a hand?' Viv couldn't help herself. She always offered to help.

Lien shook her head then leaned against the wall. 'No, I'm good, thanks. But how's things? How are you finding it?'

Viv was a little surprised by the question. 'It's great. I'm loving it.' She gave a shrug of her shoulders. 'Obviously it will be better when there's a permanent obstetrician. But the closing date has passed, and Duc said he'll look at the applications tonight.'

'Yeah, Duc.' Lien kept smiling, her eyes fixed on Vivienne. 'How long have you two been friends exactly?'

There was something about the way she said the word *exactly* that made Vivienne straighten up a little.

'Since he was a medical student.' She waved her hand. 'Not quite as long as you two, but I met Duc in his last year when he was on one of his placements in England.' She almost bit her tongue in an attempt to stop her babbling. What was wrong with her?

'Were you always so tactile?'

The question took her unawares. 'What do you mean?'

'You and Duc, you link arms, you hug, you hold pinkies.' She smiled and wagged her finger at Viv. 'It seems so natural to you both. Don't think I haven't noticed.'

Viv frowned. 'It is. It always has been.'

Lien gave a careful nod. She bit her bottom lip. 'You've never thought about doing anything more? Becoming anything more?'

Viv leaned back. It wasn't like people hadn't asked questions about their closeness before. But she'd always laughed it off with a wave of her hand. And being asked about it in the middle of the treatment room seemed odd.

'He's my best friend,' she stumbled.

Lien had the most careful expression on her face. Vivienne knew that her and Joe had recently married. They were a perfect match. Maybe she was one of those people that just tried to match up all those around her?

But even as she had that thought, somehow, Vivienne knew Lien was nothing like that.

Lien kept pressing. 'Do you ever think it was meant to be more than that?'

Her dark eyes met Vivienne's gaze steadily.

It was like a ripple of breeze from the sea back home had just jumped across the ocean to prickle her skin. She wasn't quite sure how to answer that question. But Lien's gaze was unwavering. It seemed that not answering wasn't an option.

Viv knew she wasn't jealous. Lien had her own husband and her own ready-made family. But she'd gone to medical school with Duc and had worked with his parents. Of course she would be protective of him.

Maybe she was worried that Duc was vulnerable right now. Maybe, if the shoe were on the other foot, Viv would be the one asking the questions.

Her stomach rolled over. The fleeting imaginary thought of Duc and Lien didn't sit comfortably with her at all. Even if it wasn't remotely possible. What on earth was wrong with her?

A bead of sweat seemed to form instantly between her shoulder blades and snake its way down her back. 'Once you take that step,' she said throatily, her voice shaking just a little, 'you can't go back.'

Lien licked her lips. Her gaze felt like some kind of laser beam cutting into Viv's brain, exposing all the mixed-up thoughts and feelings she'd had for the last few weeks. 'No,' she said carefully. 'You can't.' Her voice was clipped. She nodded her head at Viv, then put her hands on the trolley and turned and walked out.

Duc sifted through the application forms. Sen had written some notes on the top corner of each. She'd double-checked their résumés and their references. He couldn't help but wonder who his mother would have picked to work alongside, who would have met her seal of approval.

He sighed and leaned back. His mother had had things down to a fine art. She'd never offered someone a job then changed her mind when she'd actually met them. It was like she'd had a sixth sense for who would be a good fit for May Mắn. And Duc just didn't have that.

He didn't want to make a mistake. This was a crucial post. It was essential he get this right.

He needed someone else's opinion on this. Someone who was grounded. Who could see past the padding on a CV. He smiled. There was one person he knew who could always cut to the heart of the matter.

He looked out of the window. Viv wasn't working today. She'd gone shopping to the local market, offering to buy them both something for dinner. He got up and walked over to the bungalow, quickly changing into a loose, long-sleeved top and a pair of jeans.

He wandered through the streets, searching above the milling heads. There. A flash of the telltale red.

She was haggling with the fish seller. The old man was looking at her in complete amusement as she spoke Vietnamese with a very Scottish accent. She was gesturing with her hands, and he could tell the seller was, in part, mesmerised by her. Just like a few others round about.

Viv was wearing skinny jeans and a white long-sleeved tunic top. Her hair was loose around her shoulders, reminding him of a picture of Guinevere from a childhood storybook.

She finally pulled some money from her pocket, shaking hands with the man with a broad smile on her face.

'I take it you just used your Scottish charm?'

She jumped at the sound of his voice. 'Where did you spring from?' But before he got a chance to answer, she raised her eyebrows. 'And, no, I didn't use my Scottish charm. I decided to just be crazy Scot number one—that is what you've been calling me, isn't it?' She planted one hand on her hip.

The man behind her started to laugh, shooting a look at Duc as he handed over her fish wrapped in paper.

Duc pulled a face, cringing. 'Okay, busted. But, hey...' he held up his hands in defence '...at least I made you number one instead of number two.'

She shook her head and put the fish in the bag that she carried. He leaned in for a closer look. She'd managed to find some fresh vegetables and spices too.

'Looks great. What's for dinner?'

'Aha.' She smiled. 'It's a secret recipe.' They started walking back down the crowded street.

Duc was definitely surprised. 'You have secret recipes?'

'You know.' She shrugged. 'It's a secret to me too. I'm just going to bung it all in the wok and hope for the best.'

'How about some wine?' He steered her into a nearby store. 'Or some beer?'

Viv gave a shrug. 'Whatever.'

Duc grabbed a bottle of wine and a few bottles of beer. As he paid for them, he noticed Viv watching him, biting her bottom lip. 'Something wrong?'

She jerked, as if she'd been caught doing something she shouldn't. 'What? No.'

He shook the strange feeling off and joined her back in the street. 'I was wondering if I could ask a favour?'

She groaned. 'You want me to do the night shift again.'

He shook his head. 'No. And thank you for the night shifts you did do.' Not only had she helped with the large sick family—who had all recovered well—she was also more or less on call every night in case a woman arrived in labour. He spent most days just relieved that she was there. 'What I was actually wondering was if you wanted to interview with me for the new obstetrician.'

Her footsteps faltered. She stared at him. 'What? Me?'

He nodded. 'Who else knows exactly what we need? I've got two potential candidates that we can interview via a video call. Will you help me?'

She paused, and he could see her biting the inside of her cheek. 'What's a consultant obstetrician going to think about being interviewed by a midwife?'

Duc shrugged. 'Who cares? He or she needs to know that we are a team here. The normal hierarchy doesn't apply.'

She gave him a stunned smile, then gave an appreciative nod of her head. 'Actually, I'd love it. Can I prepare some questions?'

'You can prepare *all* the questions.'

She nodded. 'Okay, then, let's find May Mắn an obstetrician.'

She'd changed back into her denim shorts and had thrown all the food into the wok, where it was currently sizzling. Nothing had turned black yet so it seemed as though dinner might actually be a success. Duc had appeared and was watching her with unguarded amusement. He'd changed into a fitted black T-shirt and jeans. The clothes seemed to hug his frame, highlighting his broad shoulders and the planes of his chest. She couldn't help but notice the way the jeans moulded to his thighs and heat flooded her cheeks as she realised what she was thinking.

She tugged at the bottom of her own denim shorts. Maybe they were too short? She was so used to being casual and comfortable around Duc that she hadn't really given the clothes she wore much thought.

'Is this the first thing you've managed to cook without burning?' he teased.

She shot him an indignant look. 'I can burn it anytime. Just say the word. In fact...' she waved her hand '...make yourself useful and get me a beer.'

He cracked open the beer bottles and watched as she put the food into two bowls and carried them over to the table. It was odd. She was so conscious of his eyes on her. It wasn't like Duc hadn't looked at her before, but something in the air had changed between them. It was like someone had found a dial and turned it up a few notches.

She grabbed for her beer as soon as she sat down, folding one knee underneath her. Lien's words were still banging around in her head. She'd always laughed off any comment that anyone made to her about her and Duc. But this time she didn't want to laugh it off. Because it had made her brain spin.

She pushed a sheet of paper in front of him. 'Here, some sample questions. I wrote them while you were in the shower.'

He ran his eyes over them, elbows leaning on the table, a beer in one hand and a fork in the other. He took a bite of the stir-fry and looked up.

'What?' She hadn't tried it yet.

Duc stood up silently and walked to the cupboard, grabbing some spices and some soy sauce. He added some to both of their dishes, gave them a stir and sat back down. This time, when he lifted the fork to his mouth, he didn't baulk in the same way. He gave her a smile. 'It was fine.' He smiled, clearly hiding the fact he wanted to laugh. 'Just missing some taste.'

Viv bent forward. It did smell more appetising now. She took a bite, and bit her tongue on the snarky reply she'd planned. This was good.

'I've arranged another call tomorrow with Ron Jung, our advising obstetrician. It will give you a chance to review some of the patients with concerns again. He's been so good, but we can't keep relying on him permanently. We need to appoint someone soon.'

'Yeah.' Viv leaned her head on one hand and started twiddling a bit of loose hair. 'What do you think of him?'

Duc looked up, a little surprised. 'Ron? He's fine. Worked with my mother years ago. She spoke highly of him.'

Viv looked thoughtful. 'Have you ever thought of poaching him?'

'What?' Now he just looked confused.

'Poaching. Stealing a doctor from elsewhere. Happens all the time.'

Duc put his fork down. 'You want to steal Ron? Why? He's worked at the national hospital for years. He's never expressed any interest in working somewhere smaller— much smaller. He has a whole department and a salary to match. Anyhow, what's wrong with the two candidates we have for interview? I thought they looked quite good.'

Viv leaned back, stretching her arms across the table. As she stretched, her short loose top crept higher and she only realised when she saw his eyes staring and lingering. She pulled them back with a bump. 'Yeah, about them…'

'About them, what?'

'The first one will never stay. Just from the application form they've applied on a whim. Plus, he seems to go from job to job, never really staying anywhere.'

Duc's eyebrows rose. 'Sounds like someone else I know.'

Viv shot him a glance but ignored him. 'That's not what May Mắn needs right now. Not the staff and not the patients. They need an obstetrician who's here for the long haul.'

'And the other candidate?'

'Doesn't have any special knowledge about the issues in Vietnam.' She put her hand on her chest. 'A bit like me. We can't rely on Lien or you to tell us about the most prevalent conditions all the time. We really need someone that knows about malaria, TB, dengue fever, Zika and chikungunya.'

Duc looked her straight in the eye. 'Someone like Ron?'

She took a sip of her beer. 'Someone like Ron.'

'But what makes you think he might even be interested?'

Viv leaned back and smile. 'My intuition. Managing a big department isn't all it's cracked up to be.'

Now Duc smiled. He loved the way the Scottish words and expressions were scattered throughout her language.

She kept going. 'He has a huge team. Twelve consultants—twelve egos to manage. He's getting older. He's just had his first grandchild. He's already told me he wishes he could spend more time at home.'

Duc stirred at his food with his fork. It was clear he was thinking about what she was saying.

She opened her hands out. 'Why does anyone want to be a doctor? To help people. To make a difference. What if we could offer Ron a chance to finish off his career, with a bit more time at home, along with caring for those who need it most?'

Duc shook his head. 'It would be a huge salary drop.'

'You're telling me that Ron doesn't already have his pension plans sorted out?'

Duc pulled a face. 'True. Knowing Ron, he's had that sorted out since he was twenty.'

Viv leaned forward. 'I just get a feeling when I talk to him. He's been consulting with us free. But he's genuinely interested in the work that we do here. He's been so enthusiastic about some of the cases—both the ordinary ones and the complicated ones.' She played her trump card. 'His mother grew up in the same street as Lien's parents.'

Duc's eyes widened. 'Really?'

She leaned forward even further. 'Really. I think he has a vested interest in this area. How about we both do the consultation tomorrow? We could sound him out?'

For a second he said nothing and after a moment she realised just how far forward she had leaned, and that Duc had a clear uninterrupted view of her cleavage. Her automatic reaction was to pull back, but something stopped her.

Duc hadn't looked away.

Her skin prickled. Under normal circumstances both of them would have moved and thought nothing else about it. But Duc's eyes were firmly fixed on the result of her folding her arms across her chest and leaning forward, allowing her V-neck top to dip a little lower than it should.

A crazy surge went through her.

She winked. 'And see if I'm just crazy Scot number one or not.'

Duc's hand jerked at her voice, knocking the bottle of beer she was holding loosely, sending the whole thing tipping towards her.

Viv jumped up, but not before the pale amber liquid was halfway down her top and shorts.

'Sorry!' he said quickly, standing up and following her as she ran over towards the kitchen sink, grabbing a tea towel to try to wipe away some of the damage. He lifted his hands automatically to help, grabbing a roll of kitchen paper towel.

As she lifted the tea towel away it was clear her top was sodden and was clinging to her like a second skin.

Duc started patting her down with the paper towel. He started at her waist and abdomen, and then moving up to her breasts. He seemed to be on autopilot, trying to right his mistake without thinking too much about his further actions.

As his hands brushed against her breasts, she stopped breathing. He was only inches away from her.

His hands seemed to freeze in mid-air. Almost as if he'd just realised what he was doing.

She looked at him. His dark eyes were wide.

Silence filled the air between them, but the air wasn't silent—it sizzled and crackled, brimming with sexual tension.

'Surgeons aren't supposed to be clumsy.' Her voice was barely a whisper, her eyes focusing on the hands that had just touched her.

Duc's voice was lower and throatier than she'd ever heard it before. 'Haven't you heard? I'm not a surgeon any more.'

Her eyes fixed on his lips. Her tongue came out and traced along the edges of her own, instantly dry, lips.

Her move was like a magnet towards him.

He moved forward. Just an inch. Close enough she could feel the heat from his skin. It was torture.

This time it was she who moved. Her hands automatically reached out and ran up his bare arms to his shoulders. He let out a little groan as her palms and fingertips touched his skin, and it was her undoing.

She closed the space between them, pressing her damp body next to his.

Duc reacted instantly, one hand sliding around her waist and pulling her even harder into him. There was no question what was going to happen next. No doubt at all.

And for all the shooting thoughts that fired through her head, there was one that overwhelmed all the others. *Now.*

His lips met hers greedily.

It was like a million little explosions going off in her body at once. His other hand slid through her hair, anchoring her head.

She'd never wondered what kind of lover Duc might be. But all of a sudden in a few moves she knew. Masterful. Decisive.

Her legs were shaking as she responded to his every move, matching him all the way.

Her hands slid under his T-shirt, sending shudders of desire through her as she felt the hard planes of muscle and the dark hairs on his chest. At the same time one of his hands slipped under her top and he ran his fingers up her spine.

The move set every nerve firing under her skin, and her breath caught somewhere in her throat.

He bumped her back against the sink and she pushed herself upwards, making room for him to step forward and letting her wrap her legs around his waist.

Her brain was completely lost in the moment, lost in the part frustration, part desire that had erupted from inside.

She wasn't sure what had triggered the change in them both, but from the moment she'd set eyes on him at Hanoi airport she'd just known something was different between them.

For a few days she'd told herself it was his sadness and the obvious grief that was overwhelming him, but it hadn't taken long to realise that there was something else—something underlying—no matter how much they both tried to ignore it.

But she didn't want to ignore it any more—she didn't want to pretend this connection wasn't there.

Her hands tugged at his thick hair as his lips trailed a path down the side of her neck. She could see the pulse at the base of his throat racing just as much as her own.

She tipped her head back and let out a groan as the sensations started to overwhelm her, then Duc froze.

She sensed it automatically. His muscles tensing, his lips lifting from her skin.

She opened the eyes she'd just closed. 'Wh-what is it?' she breathed. She didn't want this to stop.

Duc was still frozen, his lips just inches from her neck and his hands on her skin.

He lifted his head, his dark eyes locking with hers.

'Vivienne, what are we doing?' The huskiness was still there, but now there was a sense of something else—a sense of panic. A sense of removal.

It was like a cool breeze dancing over her skin. It would be so easy to continue. So easy just to let the heat of the moment take them and carry them on to the next place.

Right now, that was exactly what she wanted.

All her words were lost somewhere in her throat. She didn't know how to answer that question.

Her pause made him step back, taking his hands from her skin. His eyes were shot with worry and confusion.

'I'm sorry,' he said. He could barely look at her. 'I don't know what came over me. You're the best friend I've got. The last thing I want to do is anything that will affect our friendship.' His hand came up and ran through his hair—the hair that moments ago she had tangled through her own fingers.

He took another step back, his voice racked with emotion. 'You're it for me, Viv. You're all I've got left. I can't mess this up.'

'Of course.' She could barely get the words out, rejection stinging harder than she'd thought possible.

She jumped down from the sink edge and walked back over to the table. 'Let's just write it off to a moment of madness.'

His tight shoulders sagged, and his sigh of relief made her stomach twist and turn. Tears threatened, gathering in her eyes.

She turned away so she wasn't facing him. 'I need to dry off,' she said, her hands leaving the plates she'd been about to lift from the table.

He reached a hand out towards her and she flinched

away. 'I don't want this to spoil things between us. You're too important to me.'

She didn't feel important. She felt like the giant elephant in the room.

She waved her hand as she headed towards her room. 'Forget it.' She waved the hand over her shoulder. 'Tomorrow is a brand-new day.'

She closed the door behind her before he had a chance to respond. Every nerve ending was on fire.

Every part of her body was calling out to be touched by his.

Instead, she was left alone. Her knees buckled and she slid down the door, wrapping her arms around herself.

She pulled her knees up to her chest and rested her head on them, letting the tears fall down her face.

Part of what he'd said was true. Duc was the closest thing she had to family. The only difference was she'd never really told him how important he was to her. Duc had still had his mum and dad. She'd always just imagined she didn't feature quite as highly in his life as he did in hers. Best friend had been comfortable. Best friend had been manageable—at least she'd thought so.

But everything had changed. How could she forget about a kiss like that? How could she pretend it'd never happened?

She wiped the tears from her face, realising that her hands were shaking. No, her whole body was shaking. She stood up on trembling legs and ducked under the mosquito net to wrap herself in the blankets on her bed.

The air around her was clammy but she couldn't seem to retain any heat. She rested her head on the pillow.

She'd started this. She'd initiated this. She'd been

the one to step forward and slide her hands up to his shoulders.

She could have brushed off the damp shirt. She could have ignored his apologetic actions. Instead, she'd moved. She'd acted.

She'd reached out to grab the connection that had blossomed before her. A connection she rarely ever made.

Or had she ever made it?

Vivienne was very used to being alone. Very used to looking after herself. From the age of seventeen she'd never relied on another person. Living a life like that was isolating. It also meant she erected a shield to protect herself from being hurt. It made it easier to move around. Moving around, she wasn't anywhere long enough to get too attached to people or to places.

Duc was the only person she'd ever let penetrate that shield—just a little.

And right now she was regretting even that. His friendship had been the one thing she'd reached out and grabbed onto.

She couldn't tell him how she was really feeling. She couldn't tell him that from the moment she'd set eyes on him at the airport and hugged him it had felt like coming home. Home. A thing she'd never really had. A word she'd never really found a place for.

May Mắn Hospital was exquisite. The problems were sortable. The staff were welcoming. The thought of getting the chance to cover at one of the other hospitals wasn't exactly too shabby either. How could she explain that for the first time ever she felt a buzz of excitement about a place. Just walking through the corridors made her smile.

And the realisation was that a huge, huge part of that was Duc.

But now?

Emptiness rolled around her in waves.

The truth was she'd never felt so lonely in her entire life.

And that made her sadder than ever.

CHAPTER NINE

DUC WAS WALKING on eggshells and they were all of his own making. For the past two weeks Vivienne had had a grin plastered to her face as if it had been painted on there.

He'd screwed up. He'd screwed up big time.

Joe had started shooting him funny glances and Lien was being down right off with him.

In the meantime, Vivienne had been true to her word. The conversation with Ron had gone well, even though both of them had been shuffling in their seats uncomfortably. Ron had asked for a few weeks to think about things, whilst still agreeing to consult on difficult cases.

Vivienne had read him well. Duc would never have imagined asking Ron to consider a position at May Mắn. But he'd smiled when asked, nodded, and hadn't seemed at all surprised. Duc's complete dread had been the thought that Ron might be insulted at being asked to give up his position for what most people would consider a less prestigious job.

But Ron had revealed that he was ready to think about some changes in his life, and that he liked the possibility of working at May Mắn. He'd mentioned a few community outreach projects that could be developed and had asked some questions that seemed to check if he and Duc were on the same page.

Vivienne had been enthusiastic, chipping in with projects she'd been involved with in other areas, and their success rate and transferability to Hanoi.

Duc hated the atmosphere in the house between them both right now, and his biggest dread was that she might go back on her promise to stay the full six months.

They'd arranged interviews this week with another midwife. But whoever they employed wouldn't be able to replace the intensity that Vivienne felt for her job and her patients.

Duc had to try and sort things out.

Viv was finishing up in an outpatient clinic when he found her.

'Do you have a minute?'

She looked up from some notes. 'Yeah. What's up?'

He could tell she immediately thought he wanted to talk to her about a patient.

'Do you want to go somewhere this afternoon?'

The pause was agonising. It felt like asking a girl at school on a date and seeing all the reasons that she wanted to say no flit behind her eyes.

'I think we should try to get back to normal,' he said quickly.

She flinched at those words, but it was too late to pull them back. He wasn't about to tell her he'd spent the last two weeks unable to sleep because of the whole 'what if' scenarios drifting through his head.

It was like being a kid with one of those books where you got to choose what happened next.

Except...none of his choices had seemed right, even in his imagination.

'Let me take you on a tour of the city. Or a drive further out. Whatever you like. I've been a poor host.'

She was going to say no. It was written all over her face.

He watched as she bit her bottom lip. 'Or let's take some time to do what we normally do. We can catch a movie. Find a bar.'

He was getting desperate and he didn't care if she knew it.

She blinked. 'I'd rather just go for a walk around the city, towards the park maybe.'

Relief flooded through him. 'Great. Why don't we get changed and I'll meet you out front.'

He turned quickly before she changed her mind, finishing up a few things with patients, then heading back to the house to change into jeans and a light shirt.

It took nearly an hour for Viv to come and meet him. He'd started to pace outside the front of the hospital. She appeared wearing skinny jeans and a long-sleeved white top with a simple bag over her shoulder and a pair of sunglasses nestled in her hair.

'You came.'

'I came,' she sighed. He could tell she wasn't exactly happy, and he wasn't used to Vivienne being like this. Normally things were so easy between them. They got to be themselves, without any need for other faces.

He wanted to reach out and touch her. But every molecule in his body told him not to. Told him that reaching for Viv again could set off a catastrophic chain of reactions that his body would want to react to.

'Let's go this way,' he said quickly. 'It takes us through the Hoàn Kiếm district and will lead us down towards the lake.'

She started walking. He was sure he should actually be leading, but Viv's long strides made him wonder who exactly was leading who here.

He kept up and started pointing out part of the city. 'This is the local school. There are more than four hundred pupils. This is where Lien and I went to school together.'

Her head turned towards him. 'You went to school together? I thought you met at medical school?'

He shook his head. 'We did both. You know Lien's parents stay just a few streets away?'

She nodded and he continued. 'They've always lived there. My parents and I originally stayed in an apartment further into Hanoi. They didn't build the bungalows until after they took over the hospital.'

They wandered through the streets. The walk from the hospital to the lake took around an hour.

Duc kept talking, partly because he couldn't stand any silence between them. It was easy to chat as the area on the way to the lake was full of shops.

Duc pointed down various streets. 'Things get a little quirky around here with each street having specific kinds of stores. Look, this street is mainly book stores. The one to the left, that's all shoe stores.'

Viv nodded and stopped to look in a few windows. She picked up something with an international brand. He nudged her and shook his head. 'This is a tourist area. That's not likely to be real.' She gave a little shrug of her shoulders. 'But it's right in my price range.' So he waited while she pulled some money from her jeans pocket and paid.

As they moved along there were vendors at various

street corners selling fresh fruit and they stopped to pick some up.

The traffic was chaotic, the streets packed with cars and mopeds, and it took an age to cross some of the roads en route to the lake. As they walked down one street they saw a bride getting her picture taken on the steps of a grand hotel. Duc smiled. 'That's one of the most luxurious hotels in Hanoi.'

'It certainly looks grand,' murmured Vivienne as she stopped to watch the bride and groom posing together. Duc didn't want to hurry her along, so he waited while photographer posed the couple on the steps. Even from here, he could tell just by the way they looked at each other that they were totally in love.

An uncomfortable prickle ran down his spine. Viv had stopped watching them and was staring at her feet. Images shot into his brain. He could remember exactly the expression in her blue eyes that night, and if he closed his eyes he could remember exactly how much his heart had thudded in his chest and exactly how much he'd wanted things to go further.

Was he a fool?

She was quite simply the best person he knew. But there was no way he could have a fling with Viv and still retain the closeness of their friendship. Even now, he'd probably gone some way to ruining it.

Everything he did now had to try and pull things back.

He gave a tug at her elbow. 'Let's go around the corner. There's some gorgeous architecture. The Hanoi Opera House is there.'

They walked to the opera house and he noticed Viv

tugging at her top. The temperature was rising, and he could see her hair sticking to her neck.

'Let's stop for a minute and get a drink before we head to the park.' He ducked into a doorway and led her to an elevator that took them four floors above the streets. 'Café hopping is almost a trend here.' He led her to a table in a café overlooking the streets below, with a view of the lake. He handed her a menu, which she handed back with her eyebrows raised.

'Sorry.' He shook his head as he realised it was in Vietnamese. 'What would you like?'

'Frozen mango smoothie,' she said promptly, and when the waiter approached, he ordered two.

He pointed down at the busy road and crossing beneath them. 'This is Hanoi's answer to Times Square or Shibuya Crossing. I could people-watch up here for hours.'

Viv leaned back in her chair. Her gaze had narrowed. 'So, are we going to talk about things or are we just going to ignore them?'

He started. He hadn't expected her to say anything quite so blunt, but this was Viv and he should have known better.

His cheeks flushed and he shook his head. 'I'm sorry. I feel as if I took advantage of you. You've came here, given up a job and everything to help me out, and then... that happens.' He ran his fingers through his hair. 'I meant it when I said you're family to me. I crossed a line. I don't know what I was thinking of.'

For the first time since it had happened her face didn't seem quite so annoyed. She raised an eyebrow. 'I know what you were thinking of.'

The waiter placed the frozen glasses down in front of them and they both jumped.

He rolled his eyes. 'Yeah...that.' He looked up and met her gaze. 'But why? Why now? How many times have you and I got drunk together—shared a bed even—and nothing like that has ever happened?'

A sad kind of smile appeared on her face. 'Who knows? Timing? Hormones? Change of venue?' Her voice dropped. 'Change of circumstances?'

He reached across the table and grabbed her hand. 'I'm sorry. This is what I hate. I'm scared to touch you now. Scared that something that was so easy between us is now just...'

He let his voice tail off. His thumb was unconsciously making little circles in the palm of her hand.

'The last two weeks have been hard,' she said simply, and he could tell she was trying to keep her voice steady. 'I wanted to go home.'

His head shot up. 'No.'

A tear slid down her cheek. 'But I realised I don't know where home is. I don't even really have one.'

He didn't hesitate. Duc stood up and moved around the table, wrapping her in his arms. 'Home is with me, Viv. We're family.'

She was shaking now, and he hated every bit of himself for doing this to her. 'You should have told me. You should have shouted at me—yelled at me. You should have told me you wanted to leave. I am so, so sorry. I had no idea you were feeling like that.'

She gave a nervous laugh and pushed him back a little. 'How could I do that? I was the one that kissed you first.'

His breath caught somewhere in his chest. She was

right. She had kissed him first. She'd responded to his every touch. Every moment of that night was seared on his brain. But he'd wanted to take all the responsibility, all the blame for what had happened.

He could tell that right now she was struggling to keep her emotions in check, and he couldn't get past the first words she'd said—that she didn't know where home was, that she didn't have one.

It pained him that she felt like that. That sweet, sunny Viv didn't have anywhere to call home in her heart.

'We reacted,' he said firmly. 'We reacted to...' he smiled and flicked his fingers '...let's just call it something in the air.' His hands went back to her shoulders. 'But we can't let this come between us, Viv. We just can't.'

She reached up and touched the side of his cheek. It was the lightest of touches and for a split second he was taken back to that night and the feel of her fingertips on his skin. Their gazes meshed. 'No, we can't,' she whispered. For an instant he thought he could read a world in her eyes—a world of loneliness. His heart twisted for her. He wanted to fix things. He wanted her to be happy.

He could feel hormones surging through him. He wanted to sweep her into her arms and tell her that everything would be fine, that home could be here for them both. But how could he do that when he still hadn't figured out where he wanted to stay or what he wanted to do next?

The waiter appeared with a loaded tray and Duc moved to let him past, going back to his seat and putting his hands around the frozen drink. Maybe it would chill some of the heat in his blood?

The mood had changed. The strain was starting to

gradually lift between them. It wasn't entirely natural, but he could sense they both wanted to make a concerted effort to fix this. They finished their smoothies and went back out onto the busy street, dodging the mopeds and finally entering the park.

As they moved inside Duc turned towards her. 'Hoàn Kiem Lake really is the centre of everything around here. The lake and temple are probably the most famous places in Hanoi city. People come here to rest, enjoy the view, and have a chance to sit back and watch the rest of the world.'

Viv looked around. 'Or get away from the traffic,' she quipped sarcastically with a big smile. She was right, of course. The noise of the constant traffic could be wearing.

The park was dotted with people. It was busy but with enough space for everyone. 'The streets in Hanoi are always busy with motorbikes and cars,' Duc agreed. 'It's nice to get a break from it. And to see a bit of green.' He gave her a smile. 'You kind of forget you're in the middle of the city in here.'

They walked amongst the dog walkers, people sitting on benches, families having picnics on blankets and tourists snapping photographs.

'That's Jade Island.' Duc pointed to the structure in the middle of the lake. 'The red bridge is called the Rising Sun Bridge and there's a pagoda on the island. Want to visit?'

Viv shook her head. 'It looks too busy. Too crowded with tourists. Let's just walk through the park and go out the other side.'

He hesitated a second then slung his arm around her

shoulders, holding his breath. But Viv just leaned into him, letting her arm rest around his waist as they walked.

They didn't talk through the rest of the park. Each step seemed to give him more confidence. Hopefully the tension in the house would lighten. What he wanted more than anything was for things between them to get back to normal.

At least, that was what he should want. But there was a tiny little voice in his head that was out on a limb here. A tiny part of his brain that wondered, *What if?*

For the last few years he'd been so focused on being a surgeon he hadn't made room in his life for anything else. Sure, he'd had girlfriends. But only for a few months at a time. His mind was always on a million other things.

But in these last few weeks when he'd been with Viv? In any second that he hadn't been thinking about the hospital, his mind had been on her. There wasn't space for anything else. Viv had captured every part of his attention. Every cell in his body had responded to her actions. He couldn't remember ever feeling a rush of emotions like that, a connection like that. Now he was agreeing to lock all that away—to put it back in the box it had erupted out of, and not think about it any more. Could he actually do that?

The words that she'd said echoed in his head again. *I don't know where home is. I don't even really have one.*

His gut twisted with the memory that Viv felt that way. He'd been so lucky. He'd had something that she'd never experienced—a happy home life with interested and loving parents. He straightened up as they walked. It didn't matter what his confusion was. It didn't matter that every time she brushed against him, his cells exploded. It didn't matter that since that kiss he'd wanted to do it again and again and again. He had so much uncertainty in his life right now, so much he needed to sort out. Did he want to go back to surgery? Should he try and make things work at May Mắn? Could he offer her anything other than a few weeks of hot and heavy fun that could ruin the friendship for both of them?

He couldn't do that to Viv. He had to put her needs first. She needed family. She needed a friend. That was his job here.

'Want to do some sightseeing?' he asked as they emerged from one of the other park entrances.

She looked around the busy streets. 'What're my options?'

A whole host of inappropriate thoughts flashed through his head. He gave his head a shake but couldn't help but smile. He pointed in one direction. 'A few blocks west is St Joseph's Cathedral.' He looked her up and down.

'What?' she asked, putting her hands on her hips.

'You have to be dressed appropriately to get in. But you'll do. No photos inside, though.'

Viv wrinkled her nose. 'What are the rest of my options?'

Duc looked around, racking his brain. It was weird. The place he'd lived a good part of his life—and everything had just gone out of his head. Maybe it was because of the way Viv had tilted her head and was looking up at him?

He waved one hand. 'There are other historical touristy places. There's Hoa Lo Prison, the Vietnamese Women's Museum and the Thang Long Water Puppet Theatre.'

She folded her arm across her chest. 'You want to take me to a prison?'

He gave a shrug. 'Only part of it exists as a museum any more. What about the puppet theatre, then?'

Viv blew a dark red strand of hair from her eyes. 'Actually, let's get something else to drink. I can't believe I've only walked across a park and I feel as if I'm ready to keel over again.'

Duc shot her a sideways glance. 'Coffee or wine?'

She looked at her watch just as his phone rang. He pulled it from his pocket and couldn't help his surprise. He turned to screen towards Viv so she could see the name as he answered.

'Ron, it's good to hear from you.'

He waited, flicking it to speaker so Viv could hear too, expecting Ron to ask about a patient, but he didn't. Instead he spoke slowly. 'Duc, thank you for your offer. I wanted to call to let you know that I'll accept. I've spoken to my family over the last few days and we all agreed there needs to be a work-life balance. I also want something that will challenge me again and let me feel as if I can make a difference. May Mắn will do that for me. I can give you three days a week. And you had better keep that sparky Scottish midwife on duty. I like her. She has passion for her job and her patients. If you're happy with those terms, I'll hand in my notice today.'

Duc's mouth was hanging open. He literally couldn't believe it. Viv had moved over, leaning over the phone but pressing against his side so she could hear part of the conversation. She tried to hide her squeal as she jumped up and down.

'What was that?' asked Ron.

Duc smiled. It felt like an enormous weight had lifted

off his chest. 'That was your sparky Scottish midwife.'
He kept grinning as Viv gave him a wink and then
turned a cartwheel on the pavement, much to the amusement of some passers-by.

'Ah, good,' said Ron, oblivious to the sight that Duc
was currently seeing. 'I look forward to keeping working with you both. Email me the contract.'

Duc agreed as Ron rang off, then he turned and
grabbed Viv around the waist and spun her around.
'We've got an obstetrician!' he shouted.

'We've got Ron!' she shouted back, laughing.

Duc shook his head. 'I can't believe it. I can't believe
he's accepted and he's giving up his other job.'

Viv's eyes twinkled. 'I told you he was ready for a
change.'

'How on earth did you know?'

She kept laughing. 'Let's just call it women's intuition, which means that you had no chance of sensing
it. Now, weren't we going to get a drink?'

'Hold on,' said Duc as he grabbed his phone again
and spoke to Sen for a few moments. 'Right, contract on
its way. Let's hold him to it before he changes his mind.'

'Why would he change his mind? He's getting to
keep doing a job he loves, without the pressure of running a department and managing a dozen other doctors. And...' she put her hand on her chest '...he gets to
work with me.'

'He does,' Duc agreed. 'Lucky him.'

He slung his arm back around her shoulders. 'All of
a sudden this day seems a whole lot brighter. I've got
my best friend back, and I've got an obstetrician that we
know and we can trust.'

Viv's hand came up and interlinked with his hand on

her shoulder. He pretended to ignore the tingle that shot across his skin.

'Didn't you promise me wine?'

He laughed. 'Oh, so it's wine now? The coffee is out the window?'

Her face looked slightly more serious. 'I think we should celebrate,' she said.

She was saying the words, but he could see something else going on behind her eyes.

Home. Those words were still echoing in his head. She'd never really had a home. She'd never staying anywhere long enough to let that happen.

Something stirred inside. She'd already told him she liked it here. She'd just persuaded a top obstetrician to work for May Mắn permanently, and Ron wanted to work with *her*.

Viv might be Scottish, but was there any reason she couldn't make a home in Hanoi?

The seed started to sprout in his brain. He gave her hand a squeeze. 'Wine it is. Let's go.'

CHAPTER TEN

THE TENSION IN the house had lifted and Vivienne finally felt as if she could concentrate on her job and enjoy it. She was learning as much as she could about the health of the people in Hanoi and getting more in tune with the specific conditions here that could affect pregnant women.

Duc had started humming again. That meant he was more relaxed.

She should be happy. She should be delighted. She should be able to write off what had happened between them as just a blip.

But somewhere deep inside it felt like so much more.

One kiss had stoked a whole lot of illicit thoughts about her best friend that she was trying really hard to lock away in a box somewhere.

Every now and then they would brush against each other or she would find herself looking at him in a different way. And either of those things would send a whole host of tingles down her spine. It was as if someone had just flicked a switch in her body.

Before, Duc had stayed safely in the 'friend' category. Could she really ever feel that way about him again? Part of her was hurt that he clearly hadn't wanted things to proceed between them. No. Strike that. Part of her was devastated.

It hurt to know that he'd been the one to stop. He'd been the one to reject her.

She couldn't even explain it to herself. But the fact that it had been Duc who had pushed away. It hurt more than ever.

With the rest of the guys she'd been involved with, there had been no real expectations. Sure, she'd thought she'd had her heart broken a few times, but the truth was there had been no promises. No happy-ever-afters. All the break-ups had been inevitable. She'd gone into the relationships knowing none of these were the guy to capture her heart.

But Duc? That was different. That was a whole host of emotions and hormones for a guy she already loved and respected. A guy she laughed with. A guy she didn't hesitate to throw her arms around. This wasn't some random pick up in a club. This was Duc. The one solid relationship she actually had with a man.

And he'd kissed her then backed away.

She was trying so hard to put on a brave front and pretend that her heart didn't feel as if it had been ripped clean out of her chest.

But in order to keep things in check, she pushed all those thoughts away and jammed them in a box in her head, somewhere out of reach. She'd learned to live like this a long time ago. When her adoptive parents had gently tried to push her in certain directions. When they'd both died in quick succession and the rest of her adoptive family had kind of faded into the background. When she'd tracked down her birth parents and realised there were no happy endings. Not for her anyway.

For the most part, she tilted her chin up and smiled.

She had to. She had a job to do. The staff here were some of the nicest she'd ever worked with. She was slowly but surely tackling the language barrier. Some nights she asked Duc to speak to her purely in Vietnamese so she could practise.

She'd become familiar with the surrounding area, the restaurants, the shops, the shopkeepers, the local transport.

The city was bright, colourful and vibrant and she felt surprisingly safe for a foreign girl in a strange place.

Some things didn't change, of course. She still burned everything she attempted to cook.

Duc still laughed at her regularly as she set off the smoke alarm in the house and had to open the doors and windows to let the smoke out.

Three months, that was how long she'd been here now.

Ron had served his notice at the obstetric hospital and had started with a bang. It had taken him five minutes to get on board with some of Joe's ideas about community clinics, and she'd found herself screening pregnant women alongside school-age children who were coming for vaccinations and older people getting treated for long-term health conditions.

He'd agreed with all the protocols she'd started within the hospital and helped oversee staff training.

She'd just gathered some notes for the clinic this afternoon when Sen appeared at the door with some letters in her hands. 'Oh, sorry, I was looking for Duc.'

'He's gone to see a patient. Someone with suspected appendicitis, I think.'

Sen gave a nod. 'I printed out the emails he asked for. I'll just leave them on the desk.'

She disappeared and Vivienne glanced at the pile of papers. Something caught her eye and she froze.

She didn't mean to read a private email—but it was just sitting there and Sen had already seen it.

It was formal, thanking Duc for his enquiry, with a string of dates and steps he'd have to take if he chose to go back to his surgical position.

He hadn't mentioned a single thing. Not once.

She looked further down the page. Duc had only sent the original email a few days before.

She gulped. He was planning to go back to his job. It was hardly a surprise. He'd always said he didn't want to stay at May Mắn permanently, and this would only ever be a temporary solution.

Her mouth was dry. But he hadn't mentioned it to her. He hadn't said anything at all.

She took a deep breath. She had a job to do. She had to get on.

She'd only taken a few steps when she heard a screech and a loud bang outside. She didn't hesitate but turned and dropped the notes back onto the main desk and ran down the corridor. Two of the nurses were already at the main entrance.

Viv ran up behind them and stared at the disaster outside.

A lorry was on its side. The front of the lorry looked as if it had hit the side of a crumpled car. The traffic outside the hospital had come to a complete halt with only a few mopeds snaking past.

She ran outside with Lien and the two nurses hot on her heels. She dropped to her knees on the road, bending down to look through the broken glass at the driver. His leg was twisted at an ugly angle and he was unconscious. She put her hand under her scrub top and punched out some of the shards of glass, so she could reach inside and feel for a pulse and check for breathing. He had one, and his breathing seemed steady.

Lien shouted over to her, 'I've got a heavily pregnant woman here. Do you want to swap?'

Viv nodded but as she turned to move away a flash of red caught her eye. Her heart rate stuttered. She knew what she was seeing. A small leg under the wheel of the truck.

'Lien!' she screamed. 'I think there's a kid under here.'

Duc appeared at her back, closely followed by Joe. They exchanged glances and Duc dropped to his knees and partially disappeared beneath the twisted metal. He looked up and spoke a few whispered words to Joe.

The nurses had run back inside to grab some supplies, and they reappeared, one with a mobile trolley and one with a wheelchair.

Joe's face was serious. 'Viv, you swap with Lien. Shout for me if you need a hand. Duc and I will take care of this.'

Her heart twisted in her chest. She knew they were trying to protect her, and a grateful part of her brain kicked in. She was primarily a midwife. She wasn't a children's nurse. Could she even be useful to them anyway?

Lien was still at the other car. She gave Vivienne a nod and they both ran, swapping places.

The little red trouser leg had imprinted itself on her brain and it took all her strength to focus on the woman in the car in front of her. She wasn't just pregnant. She was *very* pregnant.

Viv spoke in her best broken Vietnamese. 'I'm Viv. I'm a midwife at the May Mắn Hospital. How many weeks are you?'

The woman had both hands on her stomach and tears running down her face. 'Thirty-nine,' she breathed. 'But my waters have broken.'

Viv looked further into the car. There was a damp patch on the front seat between the woman's legs. Viv turned to one of the nurses. 'Can I have a BP monitor and a stethoscope? And a portable Doppler.' The woman had the window down in her car, and Viv reached her hand in to release the door. The worst impact had been on the other side, so thankfully the door opened with a couple of tugs.

She bent down next to the car so she was down at the woman's level. 'What's your name?'

The woman winced for a second.

'Labour pain?' Viv asked.

The woman nodded, her face contorting for a few seconds. 'Tho,' she breathed. 'My name is Tho.'

Viv nodded as one of the nurses ran over with the equipment. 'Okay, Tho, I'm going to check you over before we move you from the car. First thing...' She struggled, trying to find the words she needed, then catching sight of Mai Ahn waved her over. 'Sorry,' she apologised. 'Can you ask if she has any pain or numbness, in her neck or back or legs—apart from her labour pains, I mean?'

Mai Ahn looked startled by the last remark but collected herself and asked the question.

Viv grabbed hold of one of the other nurse's arms. 'Can you get me a neck collar from the orthopaedic clinic?' It wouldn't be as good as the ones that paramedics normally had in their ambulances, but hopefully it would immobilise Tho's neck enough for them to safely move her. She could hardly give birth in a car.

Mai Ahn turned back. 'No unexpected back pain, and she can move her legs and hands with no problems.'

'Thank you,' Viv breathed. She wound the BP cuff around Tho's arm and slipped a probe on her finger to check her pulse. Both were a little faster and higher than she'd expect—but then again, Tho had just been in a car accident.

'What happened to the child?' Tho asked. Tears were still falling down her face.

Viv glanced over her shoulder. Lien was dealing with the man in the upturned lorry, and both Joe and Duc were practically underneath the wheel arch, blocking her view completely.

Tho started babbling and Viv lost track of her words. Mai Ahn saw the distress and looked at Viv, asking for permission to come back over. Viv nodded, mouthing the word *please* at her.

Viv lifted the portable Doppler and waited a few moments until Tho had finished speaking to Mai Ahn.

Mai Ahn kept her face neutral. 'A little kid ran in front of first her car, and then the lorry. They both swerved to avoid him. She wants to know how he is.'

Impatient horns started to sound around them. Viv glanced up. The traffic was tailing back in every direction. She ignored it and nodded. 'Can you tell her that our doctors are looking after him, and that I'm going to listen to her baby now?'

She was always going to check on the health of the baby, but right now she was glad of the distraction for Tho.

Tho nodded and pulled her top up slightly. It only took Viv ten seconds to locate a heartbeat. She gave Tho a reassuring smile. 'It sounds good. But let's get you into the hospital, then we can contact your family.'

Tho looked relieved and Mai Ahn added another few words.

One of the nurses came over with a wheelchair. 'One minute,' said Viv.

She ran over to Lien. 'I want to move my pregnant woman. She's in active labour, her waters have broken but she's stable and I have a neck collar on her. But I'm not an expert on spinal injuries. Can you do a quick check before I move her?'

Lien nodded. 'Absolutely.'

The truck juddered and tilted towards them for a second and they both jumped. 'Sorry,' came the muffled shout underneath them.

Viv bent around the side and looked over the side of the overturned truck. Joe had his feet rooted on the ground and his back straining against the truck, giving it just a few inches of movement and allowing Duc to gently pull out the small child from under the wheel arch. Viv held her breath. The small boy was clearly unconscious, but his body and face seemed virtually unmarked. She'd been terrified about what might have been.

Sweat was coating them all. The heat outside was oppressive and as Viv turned, she saw an ice-juice cart at the corner of the street. Had that been what the little boy had been running towards?

Joe released the truck and immediately bent down next to Duc, checking the child's breathing and pulse. 'We're taking the trolley,' Duc said, waiting for Joe to come around and put his hands on either side of the child's face to stabilise his neck. Duc looked up at Lien. 'We'll send it back out for your man.'

Lien nodded and turned to Viv. 'Stay here. Give me two minutes and I'll check your woman.'

Viv gave a scared nod. Road traffic accidents weren't her thing at all. Her natural reaction had been to help. But she still felt out of her depth. She spoke a few words quietly to the man still behind the wheel. Keeping her fingers on his pulse and watching the rise and fall of his chest.

Lien was back in the promised two minutes. 'I've secured the collar and she seems stable to move. Mai Ahn will help you. Meet you back inside once I've got my man out of the truck.'

In the distance Viv could hear sirens. It was probably police. As soon as the traffic stopped in Hanoi, people called the police.

It took a few moments to help Tho into the wheelchair, with Viv inconspicuously checking there was no sign of blood on the car seat or between her legs.

It was a relief to push her back into the air-conditioned hospital.

Sen met her at the door with a phone in her hand. 'Ron said to give him a rundown. He's about an hour away.'

Viv wasn't sure whether to be relieved or offended. Sen had obviously decided to give their new obstetrician a call in case he was needed.

She was mindful of the fact this was one of his days off this week. But Ron had said he would always be flexible around his working hours—if there was an emergency, day or night, he wanted staff to feel as if they could call.

She hadn't had to do that—yet.

She let Mai Ahn take the lead with the wheelchair. 'Ron, I've got a lady at thirty-nine weeks with ruptured membranes and contractions who's just been in involved in a car accident outside the hospital. I've not had a chance to do a proper assessment. Blood pressure and pulse both slightly high, no other obvious injuries, and no sign of bleeding. Can I call you back if I have any concerns?'

She didn't want to be rude but was anxious to make a proper assessment of Tho. 'You've got it,' said Ron smoothly, as if he could read her mind. 'I'm sure you can handle things.'

'Thank you.' She smiled as she switched the phone off. It was good to know there was back-up if she required it.

It didn't take long to check Tho over. Yes, her waters had broken. Yes, she was in labour, which had started before she'd got into the car to drive to another hospital. Tho didn't stay in this area but worked in an office a few streets away. She was familiar with May Mắn Hospital and was just relieved to be somewhere that could look after her.

Viv set her up on a foetal monitor. Her blood pressure and pulse rate were slowly but surely coming down—in between contractions, of course.

Sen gave a knock at the door and Viv went out to speak to her. 'Tho's husband returned the call you made.

He's stuck in the traffic jam. Might take a while to get here.'

Viv nodded. She had to admire the woman's ruthless efficiency.

One of the other nurses came to join her, wheeling in a cradle for the imminent arrival.

Viv relayed the message to Tho, then quickly took a maternal history. There was nothing that concerned her. She spent the next five minutes doing a basic examination of Tho's body to check for any other apparent injury. Tho tugged at the collar. Under normal circumstances patients involved in an accident should have an X-ray to make sure there were no neck or spinal injuries. But X-rays weren't easy for a woman in labour.

Viv took her hand. 'I need to get one of the doctors to recheck you before the collar can come off. I'm sorry, but it's best to be safe.'

Tho pulled a face but nodded. 'Let me finish another few checks,' said Viv.

'Can you find out how the little boy is?'

Viv gave a careful nod. 'I'll let you know as soon as I can.'

It only took a few minutes to confirm that labour was indeed established and Tho was five centimetres dilated. Viv made her as comfortable as possible and, because she was unfamiliar with Tho's plans for her birth, had Mai Ahn assist in the discussion.

One of the other nurses came into to relieve her for a few minutes and Viv gave Tho's hand a squeeze. 'I'll find out what I can and see if I can find out where your husband is.'

She hurried down the corridor, searching the rooms for Joe and Duc. As she turned one of the corners she almost walked straight into Lien. 'Oh, good, the little boy, how is he?'

Lien went to answer, then put a hand to her mouth and dashed into the nearest bathroom. Oh, no. Was it bad news?

Vivienne stood for a few moments then wrinkled her nose. Her spider sense was tingling. She stuck her head around the bathroom door. 'Lien,' she asked quietly, 'is there something you want to tell me?'

Lien spun around, a paper towel at her mouth and her eyes wide.

She didn't even make any attempt to deny it. She just moved over to Vivienne. 'Please, don't say anything. Joe and I want to keep things quiet for the first few months. We've still to tell our parents, and Regan.'

Vivienne smiled and shook her head. 'Lien, your secret is safe with me.' She reached out and gave her a huge hug. 'Congratulations, I'm so happy for you all.'

Something tugged inside. She'd spent her life congratulating friends and colleagues on being pregnant. She was a midwife. Of course she loved babies. But she'd never really thought about having one herself.

Of course, at some point in the future she'd always pictured herself eventually having a family. But it had always seemed so far away.

So why now—for the first time—did she feel a pang of something else? She didn't want to acknowledge it, because then she would need to admit it was a pang of envy, something she really didn't want to admit to.

Lien nodded gratefully. 'Sorry, I think it was just the shock of the accident and the heat outside.'

'Can I do anything for you?' asked Viv.

Lien shook her head. 'No, I just want to carry on as normal. I'll grab something to drink in the kitchen.'

Now it was Viv's turn to shake her head. She took Lien's hand and led her into the kitchen and sat her down at the small table, grabbing something from the fridge, filling two glasses, then adding ice.

She sat down opposite her. 'So, we're just two members of staff who've been involved in something scary, in searing heat, who are taking a five-minute break to get something to drink.'

Lien was watching her carefully. 'What is this?' she asked cautiously as she eyed the contents of the glass.

Viv smiled. 'You can read a million potential cures for nausea online. I always recommend this one to my mums. Apple juice, ice cold. Give it a try.'

Lien took a tentative sip, gave a nod and sat back a little in her chair. She gave a little sigh and then smiled at Vivienne. 'It feels good to finally have told someone.'

Viv raised her eyebrows. 'You didn't technically tell me. I guessed.' She scratched at an itch on her shoulder.

Lien waved her hand. 'Whatever.'

'Have you seen anyone yet? Have you had a scan?'

Lien's cheeks tinged pink. 'Not officially. But Joe and I might have sneaked over the other night.'

Viv laughed. 'Well, I can complete your booking paperwork and take your bloods whenever you like. And, I can do a proper scan.' She raised her hand. 'But it's entirely up to you to decide when you want that.' She looked at Lien carefully, she seemed a little more relaxed. 'And you know Ron will see you whenever you're ready.'

'I know.' She nodded. 'Just give us a little longer.' She

gave a dreamy kind of smile. 'There's something so nice about it still feeling like our little secret.'

The look on her face said it all—the connection between her and Joe. The love. Vivienne swallowed. All of a sudden her independent streak didn't seem quite so cool. All it made her feel was well and truly alone.

She gave herself a shake. 'You feeling okay?'

Lien nodded and took another sip of the apple juice. 'There might be something in your theory.'

Viv smiled then looked around. The clinic around them was surprisingly quiet. 'Where is everyone?'

'Oh, Duc is in Theatre.'

Viv straightened. 'With the kid?'

Lien shook her head. 'With my man—the guy from the truck. He had an open fractured tib and fib. Duc's taken him in to repair it.'

'So, what happened to the little boy?'

Lien's face was serious. 'Joe's taken him in an ambulance to one of the bigger hospitals—he needs a CT scan. He had no visible injuries apart from a few scrapes. But he still hadn't woken up.'

'Oh.' Viv sagged back in her chair. 'Tho, my pregnant woman, has been asking. She's upset. She wanted an update.'

Lien frowned. 'I'm not sure that either of the drivers hit him. I think they just skidded and hit each other because they swerved to avoid him.'

'So why's he unconscious?'

Lien shook her head. 'Joe and I suspect he got a fright, fell over and hit his head. Even then, there wasn't a big lump or anything on his head. We did the Glasgow coma scale on him and he had reactions to pain. He just didn't wake up.'

Viv put her hand up to her chest. 'I'll need to find a way to tell her something. Maybe just that he's been taken to another hospital, but I couldn't see any big injuries.'

Lien nodded. 'She'll just stress otherwise. You need to keep her calm. It's hardly an ideal start to her labour.'

Viv stood up and pulled her burgundy scrub top away from her body, scratching her bare arm again. 'I think I'll just change quickly before I go back in. Still feel a bit icky.' She gave Lien a smile. 'And I've got a baby to deliver. Tell Duc to come and see me when he's out of Theatre, would you?'

Lien gave a nod and Viv grabbed her juice glass and ducked back into the locker room. She ended up taking a quick two-minute shower and pulling on a fresh pair of scrubs, tying her hair up and tucking it away.

Just as she arrived back at the delivery room Tho's husband rushed along the corridor to meet her. Viv held up her hand. 'Slow down, everything's fine.' His anxious expression instantly changed to one of relief. She smiled and held the door open for him. 'Come in. In a few hours you'll meet your baby.'

Duc pulled his theatre cap from his head. He was a general surgeon, not an orthopaedic surgeon, but the open fracture had compromised some of the man's blood vessels. If he hadn't operated, the man could have ended up losing his leg.

He made his way down to the delivery room to check on the pregnant woman. The room was buzzing. He arrived just as Vivienne was handing the newborn baby to mum. She had a glow in her eyes. It was clear that she loved this part of her job.

He stayed silent for a few moments, watching her interactions with the new parents, as a little fire came to life somewhere inside him. He couldn't help the smile that appeared on his lips.

A thought burst across his brain. He could watch her all day.

Maybe he shouldn't be thinking like this, but he couldn't help it. He'd asked her to come here and help him—and she'd done that. Now he was contemplating trying to get his old job back. The appointment of Ron was a huge factor. Ron was a safe pair of hands—someone he could trust. The new midwife from Australia would start in a few weeks too. At that point, it seemed it might be time to recruit a new doctor and get his old life back.

But even though he'd sent the emails and received a semi-positive response, something was holding him back.

And the longer he stood here, the longer he thought that thing was Viv.

All of a sudden he wasn't thinking about work any more. It would be easy to list all the ways she'd helped around here—how adaptable she'd been—not least today.

But he was thinking of all the little things, the personal things she did. The way he sometimes caught her looking at him. The way he knew he sometimes looked at her.

There it was again. The flare of attraction he kept trying to temper down. The one he constantly tried to ignore.

Just at that moment she threw back her head and laughed as the baby started to make a whole load of noises, almost as if it was having a conversation.

His stomach clenched as her gaze connected with his. For a second it looked as though she caught her breath. Then she pasted on a smile and waved him in. 'Come and meet our latest arrival.' She gestured to the parents. 'This is Duc. He owns the hospital. And this...' she smiled down at the baby '...is Tho and Jin's beautiful baby daughter.' She winked at them both. 'Can't give you a name as yet, because they were convinced they were having a boy.'

He owns the hospital. The statement made his footsteps falter.

He pushed the uncomfortable thought from his head and went over to admire the baby. He spoke in a low voice to Vivienne. 'Do you need me to do anything for you?'

She gave a shake of her head. 'Lien said we should take a precautionary X-ray once Tho had delivered, but apart from that, everything seems good.'

She lowered her voice. 'Have you heard how the little guy is?'

He nodded and gave a smile of relief. 'He woke up around an hour ago. He's developed bruises to his back and hips and an egg on his head, but he's conscious and talking.'

Her smile spread across her face and right up into her eyes. 'Oh, thank goodness. Best news I've heard.'

'Busy tonight?' The words came out before he could stop them.

'Eh...no,' she said with a wrinkle across her brow.

'Good,' he said. 'In that case, we have plans.'

He gave her a smile. Right now he had no idea what those plans might be, but he would think of something.

CHAPTER ELEVEN

'WHERE ARE WE GOING?'

'Dancing.'

'What?' Viv's face was a picture. 'You don't dance.'

'I do. Well, I do now. Let's go.'

Duc was waiting for her by the door. Her eyes ran up and down his frame. 'Are these your dancing clothes?'

He looked down at his black shirt and blue jeans and held out his hands. 'Why, something wrong with them?'

He glanced back at her. She was wearing a pair of jeans and a black shirt tied at her waist. 'Hey—we look like a matching pair!'

She pulled a face and ducked back into her room, emerging one minute later with a bright green top scattered with some sequins.

She walked over to him as she grabbed her jacket near the door. For a second he saw her biting her lip.

'What's up?'

For the briefest of seconds his gaze meshed with hers. He thought she was going to say something deep, but she just shook her head and slung her bag over her shoulder. 'A horrible accident and three, no, four patients that are all doing okay. I think our hospital might have had some good luck today.' She winked at him. 'Maybe there's some magic to the name of this place. Okay, Mr Good Luck, it's time to take Crazy Scot number one dancing.' She shot him a glance as she bopped out of the door in front of him. 'Show me your moves!'

And as she shimmied away onto the grass he thought this might have been the best idea he'd ever had.

So far, they'd been to a bar that served American burgers, then hit three different bars and had a cocktail in every one of them.

By the time they reached the club she'd was ready to move on to water. They climbed the stairs of the club. Music was thumping, it felt like the walls around them reverberated with every beat.

The club was busy and the dance floor was packed.

She stared around at the bodies jumping up and down on the floor. 'I feel old,' she said, watching the synchronised vibe around her.

Duc bent down, his lips brushing against her ear. 'What?' he shouted.

'I feel old!' she yelled in his ear.

He laughed and grabbed her hand, pulling her towards the bar, which was packed three people deep. They jostled through the crowd as the music changed to a nineties rave tune and a scream went up around them.

It seemed the old-style tunes were the favourites.

Duc's broad shoulders took him to the front of the pack at the bar and he pulled her in tight behind him, spinning around and putting a hand on the back of her waist as he bent to talk to her.

'What do you want?' His lips touched her ear again. It couldn't be helped—but neither could her reaction to his touch. Every cell in her body seemed to spring to life.

'Just water,' she said.

'What?' His brow furrowed, the music was booming around them. This time as he pulled her even closer, her whole body was pressed against his.

It was like the crowd had just moved around them, giving her no room to step backwards. As she breathed in, her senses were assaulted by the smell of him. His aftershave, the scent of his shampoo, the laundry detergent from his clothes.

One hand went automatically to his shoulder. She stood on tiptoe, reversing positions so it was she who was talking in his ear.

The cocktails were still in her system: a strawberry daiquiri, a mimosa and a sex on the beach had made her bold and a little cheeky. This time it was her lips that brushed against his ear. How would his body react? Would he react the same way that she had?

He might try to hide it, but she felt him stiffen for the briefest of seconds. It made her smile. 'Just water,' she said in his ear, lingering longer than she needed to.

Part of her was annoyed. She'd seen that email today—even though she'd no intention of mentioning it. He wanted to leave. He wanted to go back to being a surgeon.

She should be happy for him, but the truth was it annoyed her. Couldn't he see how good it was here? Couldn't he see the wonderful opportunities he had at the tips of his fingers?

Part of her was irritated by that. Duc was a smart guy—at least she'd always thought of him that way. He'd inherited not only a legacy but something he could make his own.

Viv had never had opportunities like this. The only

thing she'd inherited from her birth mother was her hair colour. She didn't even know if her father was dead or alive. She had no intention of trying to find out.

As Duc's large brown eyes stared down into hers, she thought about how life might have been if their situations had been reversed. Would she be trying to run away from ownership of three hospitals, along with the responsibility and the staff?

Maybe she would. Maybe she didn't really understand. There was no career conflict for her here. She could do the job she loved every day here—along with opportunities to learn new skills.

There was no downside.

Duc narrowed his gaze and she realised she hadn't moved. Her face was only inches from his. The last time they'd been this close…

She could see the flicker of recognition in his eyes and she quickly turned away. Last time Duc had pulled away. She wouldn't give him a chance to do that to her again.

He turned back to the bar and she pushed her way free of the crowd, standing to the side. She'd only been there a few seconds when a tall blond guy approached her. He'd had a few drinks and was in a good mood, talking closely in her ear—it was the only way to do it in the noisy club—and asking her if she wanted to dance.

She shook her head. But he didn't want to take no for an answer.

He nodded towards the dance floor as the music changed to another old tune. One that she liked. He held out a hand towards her, and after a few seconds' hesitation she took it. Why not? The electricity between Duc and her was close to setting her on fire. She had to expend her energy somewhere.

This guy was just her type. A bit merry, obviously a tourist, with no expectations of her—just like she would have none of him. Duc was planning on leaving. Why shouldn't she have a little fun?

The dance floor was busy, but not enough that she was crushed. The guy was from New Zealand. And he could dance.

Being here, in the middle of the dance floor, she could feel the energy all around her. It was electric. The guy was funny, a little drunk and he could move. She matched him, laughing away as they jumped up and down to the beat.

She couldn't remember the last time she'd been to a club and had fun like this. He grabbed one arm and spun her around, first one way and then the next.

It was fun. She was having fun. And all of a sudden she forgot about everything else.

Duc fought his way back from the crowded bar and looked around, scanning the crowd to see where Viv had gone.

He frowned, looking for her distinctive red hair. He thought she might have moved away from the claustrophobic bar and took a few steps nearer the dance floor.

He could feel the floor under his feet bounce with the movement of the people on the dance floor. Hands were in the air as everyone jumped up and down in time with a song that was distant memory from his student days. Even then, the song had been fifteen years old.

Then he saw it. The red hair swinging out wildly as Viv danced freely in the middle of the floor. She was dancing with someone. A guy with broad shoulders and blond hair. Duc felt an instant flare of jealousy.

She was laughing, the sequins on her top catching the lights in the club. It made her sparkle in the middle of the floor.

He couldn't take his eyes off her, mesmerised by the swing of her hips, the way he could see the skin at her waist as she punched her hands in the air. It had been years since he'd seen her like this. Free, laughing, enjoying life.

It was the way he loved her most.

That thought hit him like a spear through the heart.

The bottle of water nearly slipped from his hand.

It was as if all the little pieces of the jigsaw puzzle had just slotted into place in his brain.

He gave a shiver but kept watching. The guy grabbed Viv's hand and spun her round. She laughed and spun back the other way as the guy swayed with his movements.

Duc could feel his hackles rise. The guy was clearly drunk. It took every ounce of self-control not to storm over there and yank her away from him.

But what right did he have to do that? None. And Viv would eat him for breakfast.

He shook his head. He'd watched her a million times before, flirting or laughing with some guy, at times ending up in their arms—just like she'd watched him before with other girls.

Never once had it ground away so deeply in his stomach like it did tonight.

Viv twirled away, her arms in the air, sequins still sparkling. She sidled through the crowd, jigging in time to the music, back towards the bar. She spotted Duc and yelled, waving at him. The guy behind her was forgotten.

She was still dancing as she reached him, pressing both her hands on his chest. 'Come on, you promised to take me dancing!' She gave him a saucy look. 'You haven't shown me your moves yet!'

He handed her the bottle of the water. Part of him was relieved, but every cell in his body was still bristling. If Viv had put her hands around that guy's neck and started kissing him...

He put his hand around her waist. 'Think you can keep up?' he said throatily in her ear.

Her eyes were glistening. She grabbed his hands and pulled him back to the dance floor. The beat changed again, it was still fast paced—but not one of the old-type dance tunes. This was more eighties pop.

'Yeah!' Viv jumped up and down, happy with the beat. It maybe wasn't his first choice, but Duc had enough moves to match hers.

Her skin brushed against his as she twisted and turned. One kind of tension left his body, to be replaced entirely by another.

He had to keep his hands off, no matter how much they itched to touch her. They'd both had a few drinks. She was his best friend. The words continued to echo through his head.

Viv turned her back to him, lifted her arms once again and sidled backwards, still moving to the beat. As her body came into full contact with his, his hand automatically slid around to the front of her stomach. As she continued to dance, the bare skin beneath his fingers felt on fire.

He was dancing in time with her. Their bodies moving together. And he knew he should step back. He knew he *had* to step back.

But then Viv spun around and put her hands around his neck, the whole length of her body up against his. She stood on tiptoe to talk in his ear. 'Okay, so I guess you can keep up. But take me home—I'm tired.'

As her lips moved from his ear they brushed against the side of his face.

He moved. The action was automatic—he couldn't help it.

Their lips locked. Her sweet taste against him. It didn't have the same urgency as their kiss the last time. This one was different. Like a little bubble had formed around them in the crowded club—like an old-fashioned snow globe—holding them in a time and space that was just their own.

Last time it had been him that pulled away, but this time it was Viv.

Her eyes were wide, but she seemed calm. She pressed her lips together and gestured with her head towards the door.

He followed her as she pushed through the club, heading for the stairs. His brain was rushing ahead of itself, wondering what came next.

But as soon as they hit the muggy air outside, she spun around and pointed to a cart across the street. 'I'm hungry, let's get some food.'

The streets were quieter in the early hours of the morning and she darted across the road ahead of him. His heart was pounding in his chest. He couldn't read her at all.

He crossed the street and pulled some cash from his pocket, paying for the food she'd just ordered. Viv walked down the street, chatting as she ate. It was almost like nothing had happened between them.

But it had. He'd felt it. Every cell of his body was on permanent alert right now. Crying out to be next to her again.

It took him a few minutes to realise it was entirely deliberate. She was talking without talking. About the shops, the clubs, the people they worked with.

He took a few long, slow breaths. His brain was spinning. Watching her tonight had been like someone flicking a switch in his brain.

Why had they been such good friends all these years? Why had it never been more?

The swamp of caveman feelings he'd experienced in the club would never go down well with a free spirit like Viv. Truth was, he'd never felt them before—for anyone. So he was having a hard time figuring them out himself.

All he knew was that he had to speak to her.

The buzz was there. The attraction was there. He'd never wanted anything more.

She was still talking. Still filling the air between them with constant chatter.

He wanted to silence her with a kiss.

After some time they reached the outside of the hospital. She put her litter in the nearest trash can on the street and fell silent as they walked through the hospital. One of the nurses glanced at them both and gave them a knowing smile.

Did everyone see what was happening between them?

The silence echoed around them as they crossed the grass towards the bungalow. As Viv pushed open the door he started to speak. 'Viv...'

She turned and held up her hand. 'Don't.'

She walked inside and his chest tightened.

As he closed the door behind him she stood in the middle of the main room. 'Don't,' she repeated. 'We're friends. That was all. It was just a moment of madness.' Her eyes went downwards. '*Another* moment of madness.'

She stopped for a second then tilted her chin in a determined way towards him. 'It stops now. If we want to preserve our friendship, it stops now. You have one life to lead and I have another.'

Her voice shook a little at those last words then she turned, walked into her room, and closed the door.

Duc tried to breathe in. Last time he'd done this. Last time he'd been the one to step back.

But he'd stepped back without realising exactly how much his feelings for Vivienne had changed. Now they were front and centre to everything.

The closed door in front of his eyes hurt in a way he'd never imagined. He'd wanted a chance to speak to her, to tell how things had changed for him. He hadn't expected her to stop him dead. Because that was not how Viv functioned.

He wanted to throw open the door and demand that they talk this out.

But there had been something else in Viv's eyes. He'd known her too long not to see it.

She'd been happy tonight. Laughing and carefree with that other anonymous guy. When she'd come back to him, her eyes had been glistening with mischief and flirtation and he'd lapped it up, reacting to it in an instinctive way.

Because he didn't have a single doubt about what he wanted to happen next.

But Viv had looked hurt when she'd backed away. Why? This was what she wanted—and he would always respect her decision.

He breathed out, walking back over to the kitchen and pulling a beer from the fridge. As he looked around the house, he noticed things for the first time.

The shoes on the little stand in the corner of the room. The cupboard door ajar with coats hanging inside. The litter of things on the mantelpiece and side tables that were all items belonging to his parents.

For a few seconds he hung his head. He hadn't dealt with all this. And now it was time. Their clothes were still in the bedroom wardrobe. Those shoes and coats were his parents'. It was time to clear out and move on.

Viv's words about the lives they had to live echoed in his head. It had been a few months. Maybe he couldn't have faced this at first. But now it was time.

Now it was time for lots of things. And he had to make a new start.

CHAPTER TWELVE

VIV HELD LIEN's hair back while she vomited in the sink. After a minute or so she grabbed a paper towel and wiped her mouth, straightening up with a huge sigh.

'I'm sorry,' she breathed. 'It just came out of nowhere.'

Viv had kicked the treatment-room door closed so they wouldn't be disturbed. 'How often has this been happening?'

Tears formed in Lien's eyes. 'Constantly. All day and most of the night too.'

Viv frowned. 'Please, don't tell me that you've been like this since the last time I caught you being sick?'

Lien gave a sorry nod.

'And you haven't told anyone? That's been more than two weeks!' Viv sighed and shook her head. 'What does Joe say?'

Lien wiped her eyes. 'He has no idea it's this bad. I don't want him to fuss.'

Viv rolled her eyes. 'Oh, I can guarantee he'll fuss. There's a name for this, Lien. Hyperemesis gravidarum. Let me take some bloods and hook you up to an IV.' She gave a sympathetic smile and wrapped her arm around Lien's shoulders. 'You can't hide this any more. Let me take care of you.' She winked at her. 'I'm the big bad midwife. You might not know it yet, but I'm actually the boss around here.'

Lien leaned against the wall, giving another sigh. 'We've told Regan. We've told our parents. But I haven't told any of the other doctors—or the nurses.' Tears still brimmed in her eyes. 'I haven't even told Duc yet. He needs all his doctors. We're still one down.'

Viv shook her head and took Lien's hand. 'Okay, this is the point you stop being a doctor and I start being your midwife. I'm going to phone Ron. I'm going to get him to order you to stop working, get some rest, and get started on an IV. You're dehydrated, Lien. We need to get this under control.'

Lien's eyes were glassy now, but she nodded and Viv understood. She'd needed someone to take the decision away from her, otherwise she'd just keep working until she finally collapsed.

Viv opened the treatment-room door and led her through to a single side room, grabbing a sick bowl on the way. 'Have a seat on the bed and I'll get things organised. And,' she said slowly, 'I'll go and grab Joe, and tell Duc he needs to come in and see you.'

Lien nodded. She already looked secretly relieved. Then she held up her hands. 'Take my bloods first, otherwise that pair will try and do it. I'd prefer it if it was you.'

'Of course.' Fifteen minutes later the bloods were taken, Ron had consulted with them over the phone, insisting he'd be in that evening to see Lien, and the IV was in situ.

Viv walked down the corridor to Theatre and shook off the headache she was having. Last night had been weird. She'd had chills, actual chills, and had woken up sweating so badly she'd had to change her pyjamas. When she'd checked her temperature it had been high. Truth was she'd felt kind of weird the last few days. She'd hoped she wasn't coming down with something so she'd taken some paracetamol then, and a few more this morning. She still wasn't feeling a hundred per cent, but she had a job to do. There wasn't time to be sick. She pushed open the door to where Duc and Joe had just finished and were changing into clean scrubs.

'Hey, guys,' she said, as the door banged open.

Both looked up, surprised. It wasn't that she hadn't seen either of them in a state of undress before—the theatre changing room was shared. It was just unusual for her to come in unannounced.

'Something wrong?' Joe asked immediately.

She gave him a nod. 'I have a new patient in room seven. Hyperemesis gravidarum. Eleven weeks. Dehydrated and hooked up to an IV.'

Joe let out an expletive and walked straight out the door.

Duc was clearly confused. 'What am I missing? Is Ron not available?'

It was clear he was thinking about the patient and symptoms. This wasn't usually the kind of patient Viv would bring to him.

His frown deepened as he processed Joe's reaction, then she could see recognition forming in his brain. She nodded. 'It's Lien. I said I'd come and get you both.'

He finished pulling a fresh scrub top over his head. She couldn't miss the broad shoulders and abs, but she was telling herself not to look at them, just to focus on his face because that was safer. But was it?

Ever since that second kiss, she'd had dreams every

night that were filled with Duc. Every morning she woke up angry with her subconscious for letting him in. He would be leaving soon. She had to stop associating this place with him. Particularly when she liked this place so much.

The previous fleeting thoughts about this place feeling like home had been pushed from her head. She'd recognised that she'd started to associate Duc with feeling like home. That wouldn't happen. She'd been crazy to even think about things for a second. It was a waste of time and energy, and if she focused on the angry part, she could try and forget the hurt part.

Because if she thought about it too much, it played havoc with her senses. Her brain was so glad she didn't have to contemplate the thought of Duc not wanting to leave, because where would that leave her? She'd have to face up to how much her feelings towards him had changed, and what that was doing to her. Even at the club, that guy who'd asked her to dance had been her 'safe' option. The type she always chose. Because there was no attachment, no relationship potential. She could keep that shell around herself perfectly in place. But if it was Duc...

She was trying hard to keep things on an even keel between them.

Things had been awkwardly casual. It was the way it had to be.

She appreciated that he hadn't pressed her on what had happened between them. But it meant that once again there was a tension in the air between them, both of them finishing conversations as quickly as possible and moving on.

He still hadn't told her about returning to his surgi-

cal position, and she almost understood that. The old
ease between them had gone. Previously she would have
expected him to tell her almost everything. But now?
Would he be the first person she would tell about any
life-changing plans? Probably not.

Now he gave her a half-scowl. 'Why didn't you tell
me Lien was pregnant? Why didn't you tell me she was
sick?'

He'd started down the corridor with long strides and
she had to run to keep up. She grabbed his hand, making him stop. 'If I have to explain patient confidential-
ity to you, Duc, it's a bad day between us.'

There was a flash of fury in his eyes. She almost expected him to spit out, 'Isn't that normal for us now?'

Instead, she watched him take a deep breath. 'I
thought we practically had a shared brain, Viv. You tell
me, I tell you. It doesn't go any further.'

She met his gaze head on as a surge of anger pulsed
through her. She could so easily spit out that she'd seen
his email. But she didn't. She just shook her head. 'So
did I,' she said instead, and walked past him into Lien's
room.

Joe was sitting on the bed next to her with his arm
around Lien's shoulders.

He looked at Viv straight away. 'Did Ron give you
a time?'

She nodded. 'He just sent me a text. He'll be here at
five-thirty.'

Duc walked around her and bent to kiss Lien on the
side of the cheek. 'Congratulations, Mumma. Now, what
can I do to help you?'

Lien laid her exhausted head back on the pillow.
'Cover her shifts,' Viv answered for her. 'Lien needs

some time out. Sometimes this passes—sometimes it can last a whole pregnancy, and right now we have no way of knowing.'

Duc nodded. 'Fine. I had some enquiries the other day. A doctor who worked here with my mother and father wondered about coming back for a spell.'

Joe looked up. 'That would be ideal. You know that your mum and dad will already have checked them out. It would save the time of having to advertise and interview for a job.'

Duc nodded. 'I'll get Sen to pull out their file. Unless there's anything to give concern, I'll see when they can start.'

Lien's brow furrowed. 'Do you have a name? I might have been here when they worked here before.'

Duc nodded and pulled his phone from his pocket checking his emails. 'Yip, here it is. A French guy, Emile Dupont?'

Lien smiled as she closed her eyes. 'Ah, I remember him. He's in his fifties. He's a great doctor, very lyrical.'

Viv frowned. 'What do you mean?'

Lien kept her eyes closed. 'He's like a walking poet. His grasp of the language is good, and he can talk to patients for hours. They get almost mesmerised by him.' She opened her eyes for a second and met Duc's gaze. 'He's a good fit. He'll do well. I hope he can make it.'

'Consider it done.' Duc sounded determined. Viv could see the worry on his face as he looked at his friend.

She liked that about him. Part of her felt a little guilty for not telling him about Lien, but her professional head reassured her she'd done the right thing. The good thing was she was confident he would do anything he could to help Lien—as would the rest of the staff.

She gave a nod. Joe was stroking Lien's hair and she could tell they needed a little time alone. 'Hey, guys, can I pick up Regan for you at nursery?'

Joe shot her a grateful look. 'That would be great. I'll call and tell them you'll be there. Thanks so much.'

'No problem.' Viv checked Lien's IV one more time, filling in her charts before leaving the room and giving a quick handover to the nurse in charge.

Duc followed her out of the room. 'Viv.' She turned, thinking he was going to complain, but instead he gave her a grateful glance. 'Thanks for looking after Lien. I'm sorry I snapped at you. Of course you couldn't tell me, and I know she's in safe hands with you and Ron.'

She breathed a sigh of relief. 'Don't worry, Duc. If I need to consult at some point, I will.'

He nodded, reassured, then paused, and she could tell he was going to say something else. Her stomach clenched as she waited.

'Could you give me a hand with something later?'

'Sure,' she said cautiously, wondering what on earth she'd just got herself into. That headache was still nagging away at her.

'I need to have a clearout—for the goodwill store. I should have done it earlier, but I guess—' his brown eyes met hers '—I wasn't ready yet.'

She understood instantly. She knew the cupboards were still stuffed with his parents' clothes and possessions. She'd never said anything because it wasn't her issue to push. She gave a nod. 'Let me pick up Regan and I'll help you when I get back.' She turned to leave then gave a little smile. 'Stick around for a bit in case Lien needs anything prescribed.'

She knew he was frustrated about his friend and

letting him feel valuable would help them both. Joe shouldn't really prescribe anything for his wife, so until Ron arrived, Duc would be in charge.

'Sure.' He nodded and took a seat behind the desk at the nurses' station. Somehow Viv knew he would still be sitting there when she got back.

Duc was feeling odd. He supposed it wasn't unusual. He'd collected a host of boxes and bags. Viv appeared at the bedroom door, looking looked a little paler than normal. 'Let's be methodical about this,' she said. She'd changed into a pair of old joggers and an oversized T-shirt, her hair tied up high on her head. He was glad. She knew exactly how big a job this was going to be.

She went to one of the kitchen drawers, found a black marker and started writing on a few of the boxes. The word *Goodwill* adorned a few, *Keep* adorned another, and at the last second she paused, finally writing *Completed* on it.

'Okay,' she breathed. 'We'll start with the clothes. Anything that's in good or reasonable condition goes to goodwill, anything you want to keep for yourself goes in the keep box, and the rest of things, like underwear, et cetera, we'll put in the completed box.'

Now he understood. She hadn't wanted to write *Garbage* or *Disposal* on it. *Completed* was a nicer way to label all the things he'd have to take to the dump.

He nodded. She grabbed her phone and set it on the speakers. He wondered what she was doing, but then a familiar playlist filled his ears. It was songs they'd listened to across the span of their friendship. Most of them had a memory attached. But it was a memory of Viv and Duc—usually fun and light-hearted. Feel-good sorts of songs. Something to distract them while they worked. She pulled out a bowl and filled it with the chocolate they always ate in the UK.

'Where did you get them?' he asked.

She smiled. 'I had them stashed. Seemed like a good time to share.'

He leaned over and gave her a hug, not letting it mean anything more than it should. She was doing this for him.

It was harder than he'd thought. Every now and then a flash of his mum or dad's clothing would give him a flashback—a memory from the past. Several times he had to stop and just breathe. Viv watched quietly.

She was methodical, folding his mother's clothes into piles neatly in the appropriate box. He hesitated over a familiar shirt of his father's. He eventually shook his head and put it in the goodwill box along with the others.

Books were next, with him keeping a few. Then shoes which were all bagged up for goodwill too. The photograph albums he left in a cupboard. They could be done another day. Viv helped him wrap some older ornaments in tissue paper and pack them away. A few were sentimental but some could go.

He watched as she sighed as she wrapped things in tissue paper, her hands pausing. Her voice was quiet. 'Last time I did this was for my mum.'

She glanced up at him. He could see the hidden tears in her eyes. 'My adoptive mum,' she clarified. 'You think that you're ready but packing up the house is hard. It hits your gut in places you just don't expect it to.'

He reached over and laid his hand over hers for a second. He'd expected this to be hard, but he'd forgotten that this would bring up memories for Viv too.

'You don't need to help.' His voice was hoarse.

Her eyes met his. 'Yes,' she said clearly. 'I do.'

She stood and walked through to the bedroom, coming out a few moments later with his mother's jewellery box in her hands. 'What about this?' she asked tentatively. 'Will we just put it somewhere safe?'

He shook his head and held his hands out. 'Bring it here. My mum had a vast collection of jewellery, most of it just decorative. There are only a few things that are special.'

She sat next to him on the sofa and set the wooden box on his knees. Duc paused for a moment, noticing his hands were shaking. This should be routine. There were millions of people around the world who'd had to do this. He wasn't the first person to pack up the belongings of his mother and father.

He opened the box and lifted out the first item, a black jewelled necklace. It was something his mother had worn frequently because it had gone with lots of her clothes. He passed it to Viv without a word. A long silver chain followed, then a necklace with a large red charm. There were a number of bracelets and bangles. Some he didn't recognise at all, and he passed them one by one to Viv. He stopped at a tri-gold bangle, the three colour strands twisted together. He put that back in the box. It had been an anniversary present from his father.

Then there was a gold locket. He turned it over in his hands. It was followed by an emerald-and-diamond ring. His mother and father had been buried wearing their wedding rings. He hadn't thought to question where his mother's engagement ring was. He hadn't thought about it until now.

A sound caught in his throat.

Viv's hand came next to his. She intertwined their

pinkies but didn't say the words. She didn't have to. The warm feeling spread through his skin.

'Of course,' he said softly. 'She wouldn't wear her engagement ring at work. Infection control.' His finger ran across the face of the emerald with diamonds set on either side.

Viv spoke quietly. 'It's nice, you know. That you have something to cherish that belonged to your parents. Something you can keep and remember them by.' Her voice had a strange tone to it. 'I remember your mother wearing that ring on occasion. She loved it. It meant so much to her.'

He looked up to catch the expression on her face. It made him catch his breath.

The look in her eyes was distant. It wasn't envy, it was sorrow. It struck straight to his heart.

This was the second time he'd realised what he had in comparison to her. How not everyone grew up with happy memories and safe lives.

He took the last things from the box, leaving just the bangle, the locket and the ring. His eyes fell on the packed boxes covering the floor. 'I think this is enough for today.'

She nodded and pressed her lips together. 'Sometimes I wonder if you know what you've got here, Duc.'

He looked up sharply. 'What do you mean?'

She took a deep breath. 'I mean, I like this place. It's already wonderful, and you could make it even better. I haven't even seen the other two hospitals. I have no idea of the potential there.'

He was surprised. 'Viv, you almost sound like you don't want to move on.'

She stood up quickly, not wanting to get into any

conversations like this. 'You know me,' she said breez-
ily. 'I don't put down roots.' But when she swallowed
there was a lump in her throat. Even though they were
sorting through Duc's parents' things, it was hitting her
hard. It was bringing home to her just how isolated an
existence she led. Who would do this for her one day?
She couldn't even bear to think about it.

She'd spent so long being self-sufficient, not giving
any part of herself to someone else, because she didn't
trust anyone with her heart, and her life.

She blinked away the tears that formed in her eyes.
Even Duc. She'd pushed away the one person who'd
managed to break through her barriers a little.

Now it was her turn to have shaky hands. She'd seen
the relationship between Lien and Joe. It actually made
her stomach ache she envied it so much—the together-
ness. The 'us against the world' mentality of it all. Joe
had lost his first wife. How hard had it been for him to
reach out again?

She sucked in a breath through her teeth, willing it to
steady her hands and her heart rate. Tiny parts of Hanoi
had been tugging away at her heart this past few months.

She loved the people, she loved the buzz of the streets,
she loved the work. It was the first time in a job where
she hadn't started automatically looking for something
else a few months in.

But Duc was a huge, huge part of this.

Would she want to stay if he wasn't here?

His voice was quiet. 'But you can't be like that for
ever. At some point, in some place, you might find a
place that you don't want to leave six months later. Do
you think this could be the place?'

It was almost like he was reading her mind.

She looked up at him, her eyes wide. 'How can it be the place, Duc? It's yours. It belongs to you—and you don't even want to be here.'

She could feel the anger rise in her chest. 'I've told you before to look around you—look at what you potentially have. But you don't want it.' She shook her head. 'I just don't get it. Everything handed to you on a plate and you want to walk away.' Now she really was shaking all over. 'I saw the email. You didn't even tell me about it—but I know you're going back to the surgical programme. So what's the point of asking me if I want to stay when you want to run away?'

She could have asked about this earlier—she'd wanted to. But part of it had been pride. She'd wanted him to tell her himself. And the other part? That was being afraid of his answer. The reasons why he wanted to go back. She didn't need to hear that she just wasn't enough for him to consider staying.

Duc flinched. 'You think I'm running away? And you think all this came on a plate?' He flung out his hands. 'I got this because my parents are dead, Viv. Not because I chose it.' He was mad and he couldn't hide it.

But Viv didn't back down, she was too riled up. She leaned towards him. 'Well, you should. You should choose it. You should want it. Because I do.'

The words came out of nowhere from a place deep inside her and they both stopped talking and stared at each other for a few silent seconds.

Duc reached up and touched her shoulder. 'You want to stay?' His touch seemed to still her trembling body.

Panic gripped her. She'd said that out loud. She hadn't meant to, and Duc was looking at her in the strangest way...

'No,' she shot back quickly, trying to find a way to retreat. 'Of course not.'

'You do.' He shook his head. 'Admit it. You like it here. You want to stay.'

It felt as if her throat was closing over. No words would come out. She felt exposed. As if he could see inside her. She didn't like that—she wasn't ready for it.

Her head was pounding again. She stood up and walked over to the cupboard to find some more paracetamol. Duc followed her. 'We need to talk about this.'

'No,' she said determinedly. 'We don't. What difference does it make anyway? You want to leave. I want to stay. What's there to talk about?'

She popped some paracetamol from the foil and grabbed some water. Duc's eyes went to the medicine. 'What's wrong?'

She shook her head. She didn't want to discuss this with him either. But before she had a chance to respond his brow furrowed. 'Who said I was going back to surgery? I might have made a few queries, but I haven't decided that.'

She was starting to see spots in front of her eyes. 'If you're not going back, why ask the question?'

Her stomach cramped as a wave of nausea swept over her. All of a sudden she knew she needed to lie down. Maybe if she did, this headache would go away.

Duc glanced at her, a worried expression on his face as he moved closer. He sighed. 'I was keeping my options open. But the longer I stay here, the more I realise what I can do. You're right, there's a world of opportunity here. It's just taken me a while to see it. I was so set on being a surgeon that I didn't really take the time to consider other options. But now...' He let his voice tail off.

He blurred. Either that or he moved a supersonic speed. Or maybe he didn't. She was going to be sick. The tiny spots that had appeared at the edges of her vision threatened to take over.

Then all of a sudden everything went black.

The last thing she felt was Duc's arms around her as the world slipped away.

CHAPTER THIRTEEN

'What on earth happened?'

Joe met him in the corridor as he carried the collapsed Viv in his arms over to the hospital. His arms were starting to shake as Joe took part of the weight and they carried her over to a trolley.

'She had a headache. She felt sick, then she just went.'

He was as confused as Joe, trying to put the pieces together.

Joe moved straight into doctor mode—he wasn't blinded by the emotion that encompassed Duc.

'Let me check her over.' He turned, giving Duc a look that told him he expected him to leave the room, as one of the nurses rushed in to assist.

'Viv!' She gave a strangled little cry as she realised who it was, and her reaction made Duc aware of just how much the staff here loved Viv.

He took a few steps out to the corridor, staring down the hallway. The irony. Joe's wife was in a room just up the hall and officially Joe shouldn't treat her. Now Viv was in this room, and Duc knew deep down that the same rules should apply.

Joe shouted out to him, 'Go and check back in the

bungalow and see if you find any clues. Any medications. Anything that could cause this.'

Duc shivered. Did Joe think this was deliberate? No way. He ran back across the grass to the bungalow, throwing open the door to Viv's room and looking around. There was nothing. Nothing to give him cause for concern. He tripped over a pile of pyjamas on the floor and bent down to pick them up, and then he froze. They were damp. Just a little. But the temperature in here was warm, meaning they had much damper when they'd been taken off.

Had Viv had a temperature last night? Sweats? Why hadn't she mentioned it? She'd just got up and gone straight to work this morning.

Something sparked in his brain. Those paracetamol had been sitting out earlier. It was he who had put them back in the cupboard while making breakfast. She'd either had a temperature last night or a headache.

He dashed back across the grass, stopping at the door of the examination room. 'Paracetamol,' he said quickly to Joe. 'She's been taking them since the middle of the night. She said she had a headache just before she collapsed but I think she's had a temperature too as she changed in the middle of the night.'

Joe looked up, his face grave. He was at the far side of Viv. But before he got a chance to speak one of the nurses rushed down from Lien's room. 'Lien said to check her over. She said at the accident scene a few weeks ago Viv rushed out to help wearing just her short-sleeved scrubs. Could she have been bitten by a mosquito? Lien thinks she remembers seeing her scratching a few times.'

They all exchanged glances and Duc felt sick to his

stomach. He'd been there too and hadn't even considered the dangers for Viv. They'd all been too focused on the accident. Had he noticed her scratching since then?

'But I always remind her about wearing repellent. She's good at it.'

'Has she been shaking at all?'

Duc felt cold. The list of symptoms were forming in his head. 'She was trembling earlier.'

Joe pulled a face. 'There's a mosquito bite here. Right around the back of her upper arm. Impossible for her to see properly, but still somewhere she could scratch.'

He gave some instructions to the nurse. 'Get me some blood bottles and a cannula I need some ACT and a glucose drip.'

Duc couldn't help himself. 'Let me help.'

Joe looked up. 'No.'

'If it was Lien, would you take no for an answer?'

Joe paused for just a second, then waved his hand. 'You draw up the drugs while I take the bloods.'

Duc was shaking his head as he drew up the broad-spectrum antibiotic. 'How can it be malaria? It's supposed to be virtually eradicated in city areas. She's been taking her medication. I don't get it—I just don't get it.' He couldn't stop the frustration bubbling inside him.

'Virtually eradicated,' said Joe carefully. 'Not completely. And we have to treat what we see.' He finished inserting the cannula and attached the glucose drip. 'What I do see is an infected mosquito bite. Maybe she missed a dose of her medication. Maybe she's part of the ten per cent it isn't completely effective for.'

As Viv gave a few twitches on the bed, Joe kept his voice steady and calm. 'I think we have signs of cerebral oedema. You know how we need to treat this. We can't waste time fighting about it. Time is too important.'

A chill spread over Duc's body. He knew Joe was right, but he hated him right now for saying the words out loud. Duc couldn't remember the last time he'd seen a fatal malaria case—but he'd spent the last few years in the US.

He'd brought her here. He'd asked her to come. She would never have set foot in Hanoi if it hadn't been for him. This was all his fault. If anything happened to Viv, he would never forgive himself.

Her onset had seemed quick. She could have been bitten up to two weeks ago, but her actual symptoms only seemed to have been emerging over the last day or so. Just how virulent was this parasite?

'What's her blood sugar?'

Joe looked up as he pulled up a chair to the bed and turned a chart around.

Duc gulped. It was low. Malaria caused hypoglycaemia. The glucose drip should bring it up, but if she still remained unconscious once her blood sugar was corrected it meant that cerebral malaria had taken hold—and that could be fatal.

He handed over the other drugs to Joe, who started to administer them slowly. If Joe noticed his shaking hands he didn't say anything.

Maybe he should go and spend time with Lien while Joe was here, but the truth was he just couldn't leave Viv's side.

Joe caught his gaze. It was almost like he could read his mind. 'Lien's sleeping right now. The vomiting has really taken it out of her. She needs some rest.'

Duc nodded, his hand reaching across the sheet to intertwine with Viv's. She was deathly pale. It was amazing. The whole time Viv had been here her skin had seemed kind of sun-kissed. But maybe it just seemed that way because she was normally so full of life. Right now, she was paler than he'd ever known her.

His eyes fixed on the thin gold chain around her neck leading to the butterfly pendant. The one he'd bought. The one she always wore.

Her hand twitched in his. He was back on his feet in an instant.

Then her arm twitched, then her whole body started convulsing. Duc pulled her over onto her side, trying his best to get her into the recovery position. Ron appeared at the door and took one look, sizing up the scene in seconds.

'What drugs do you need?' he asked Joe.

Joe rattled them off and Ron reappeared in the blink of an eye. 'Let me help,' he said. Joe was trying to support Viv's airway as Duc kept a firm hold of her twitching body. He'd glanced at the clock as she'd started and was praying this wouldn't last more than a minute. His head was close to her hair and the orange scent of her shampoo was filling his senses. He felt panicked. He'd only just realised that he loved her, and he hadn't had a chance to tell her yet. To tell her that he'd been thinking about nothing else.

He'd thought there was time. He'd thought there was plenty time. He'd been figuring out about the job—and she'd challenged him in that too. Viv seemed to know his life before he did.

He'd just decided to turn down the position he'd been offered. He could still be a surgeon and work here. But he could also be a doctor. A person who worked with the most disadvantaged population on a daily basis.

The thing that had driven him to go to medical school. He'd forgotten about it for a while, getting caught up in the bright lights and competitiveness of the surgical rotations. It had taken all this for him to realise he should take another breath, reassess.

All the things that Viv had said to him.

Viv, the woman he was holding in his arms. The woman that he loved. Maybe he'd always loved her and had just been afraid to say it out loud. Or maybe it was just the change of time and conditions for them both.

Whatever it was, it was here. It was now. And, as his gaze flickered to Joe and he could see the worry in his colleague's eyes, his heart plummeted.

He could only pray he'd get a chance to tell her.

Ron came around and held her arm firmly to access the cannula and insert the drugs. Worry streaked across his forehead. 'When did Viv become ill?' he asked.

'In the last hour,' said Duc, his voice cracking. 'We think she may have been bitten when she helped at the RTA the other week. But she only complained of a headache today.'

'That's all?' Ron's brow remained creased.

'I think she was having night sweats too and just didn't say anything. I found her nightclothes back in the bungalow.'

Ron winced. 'A sudden onset, then.' The words struck them all, and they exchanged glances. They all knew exactly how serious that could be.

'Has she been taking anti-malarials?'

Duc nodded. 'Religiously.'

'Could be a resistant strain or a new one?' said Ron

thoughtfully. Viv's body started to cease twitching, the movements becoming smaller and less pronounced.

There was a collective sigh of relief.

'Did you take bloods?' Ron queried.

Joe nodded.

Ron straightened. 'Let me follow them up. I have connections at the city lab. I can get them fast-tracked and see if there is anything else we can start her on.'

As he headed to the door he stopped and put a hand on Joe's shoulder. 'Give me five minutes and I'm all yours. We'll get Lien sorted too.' He gave him a smile. 'Congratulations.'

Duc felt numb. Of course. He should be celebrating his friends' good news. But somehow that had gone completely out of his head. One of the nurses appeared at the door with a cardiac monitor and BP cuff on a portable trolley. Duc rolled Viv onto her back and let the nurse attach them. 'I'll stay with her,' she said.

But Duc shook his head. 'No. I will.' He sat down by her bed and took her hand again, raising his gaze to Joe. 'Thank you.'

Joe nodded. 'I'm just down the corridor. Shout for me anytime.'

'Me too,' reiterated the nurse.

They both left, leaving the only noise in the room the sound of the monitor and Viv breathing.

Duc leaned forward and brushed a strand of her hair from her face. He couldn't believe this had happened. All his fault. If he'd never asked her to come here, she would be back in England somewhere—somewhere safe.

Her skin was soft to his touch. 'Wake up, Viv,' he whispered. 'Please, wake up. Wake up and I'll do anything you want. I'll give you anything you want.'

Her breathing continued, steady and calm. He'd thought the worst day of his life had been the phone call about his parents, but now? This was a close rival.

He intertwined his fingers with hers. 'I can't lose you, I just can't.'

Nothing mattered more to him right now. Nothing at all. The pulse of attraction that had buzzed between them. The kisses they'd shared. The fights. All he wanted was his Viv back.

But as he looked at her lying on the bed, so pale she practically matched the sheets, his guts twisted.

There might be chance that wouldn't happen.

He adjusted their hands so their pinkies intertwined. 'Friends for ever,' he whispered.

CHAPTER FOURTEEN

HE STAYED THERE for two days and two nights, terrified that if he left something else might happen.

Her blood-sugar readings came back to normal relatively quickly. But still she didn't wake up.

The staff was great. He still had a job to do, so they would bring him charts to sign along with cups of tea and snacks. Joe brought him in a towel and a fresh pair of scrubs with a pointed nod, so he used the shower in the bathroom attached to Viv's room so he wasn't too far away.

Lien was still unwell too. It was unlikely she'd be able to resume duties anytime soon. That didn't stop her wheeling her IV down the corridor and coming in to speak to them both, clutching a sick bowl in one hand.

Ron had been as good as his word. Viv's bloods had been fast-tracked and after a quick consultation with another expert they'd started her on an alternative medication. Right now, Duc would try anything.

It was late at night. Duc had pulled in a more comfortable chair so he could sleep next to her bed. It was the kind that could recline and even though the nurses could do it in the blink of an eye, it always took him about five minutes to figure it out.

Just as he finally managed to push it back there was a little moan from the bed.

He froze. And spun around.

It was the first sign of anything from Viv in two days.

He leaned forward, grasping her hand again. 'Viv, it's Duc. Can you hear me?'

Nothing. His eyes went to the monitor, willing the heart rate to speed up to give him some kind of sign that she was listening, that she was hearing him.

But it just continued to blip along.

Frustration gripped him and all the while he told himself to remain calm. It was *something.*

After hovering over her bed for an age, he finally settled down into the chair beside her bed. 'I'm here, Viv,' he said quietly. 'Whenever you need me, I'm here.'

Sleep finally claimed him but he woke in the early hours of the morning. He sat straight up, wondering what had woken him. It was dark outside with only a smattering of stars in the sky. He frowned, straining to hear any noise in the corridor outside. Had it been one of the nurses? A phone perhaps?

He pushed the chair forward, planting his feet on the floor.

There was a noise, a groan again and he was instantly on high alert. 'Viv?'

Her nose was wrinkled. 'Headache,' she croaked.

'Brilliant!' he shouted, leaning over and gathering her up in his arms. Her body was still weak, and she didn't return the hug. He pressed the nurse call button.

'You have no idea how worried we've all been,' he breathed. 'I am so, so sorry.'

It was almost like she wasn't really processing his

words. 'Headache,' she repeated as she sagged back into the pillows.

The nurse appeared at the door, her eyes wide. 'She's awake?'

He nodded. 'Just. Can you get Viv something for a headache?'

The nurse nodded and disappeared, coming back a minute later with a glass of water with a straw and a couple of pills.

'Let's try these first.'

Duc wound the bed up and helped Viv adjust her position so she could take a tiny sip of water. She coughed and spluttered. She still hadn't really opened her eyes.

He tried to move into doctor mode and ask a few standard questions, but her replies were distinctly groggy.

He knew her body was hydrated because of her IV, but she still hadn't drunk any fluids in two days.

After a minute or so she held out her hand for the tablets and swallowed them awkwardly. Her eyes closed immediately.

Duc wanted to shake her, to make her try and talk again, to see what else he could do. But the nurse shot him a warning look. 'Our patient needs rest. Take it from someone who's had malaria.'

He pushed himself to give her a smile. She was right. He knew she was right. But so much was bubbling inside him right now.

She headed for the door. 'I don't suppose there's any point in me trying to persuade you to spend the night in your own bed now that she's woken up?'

He shook his head. 'None at all.'

She shook her head too, giving him an amused smile. 'Didn't think so.'

* * *

Her head was fuzzy. And not a good kind of fuzzy. Somehow this felt like the worst hangover on the planet; in fact, she'd never actually had a hangover this bad.

And she was tired. Really, really tired. This didn't feel normal.

She turned around in her bed, wondering why she couldn't get comfortable. The sheets were stiff. So was the pillow. Had Duc changed her bedding?

Her eyelids flickered open. White. Everywhere. That wasn't right. She'd grown used to the pleasant washed-out red of the walls in Duc's house.

If she had the energy she'd sit up. But she didn't.

Then she saw Duc in a chair next to her. Why would he be sitting by her bed? He looked terrible.

She didn't even need to speak because his eyelids flickered open and he jerked then leaned forward, grabbing her hand. 'Viv, you're awake. How are you feeling?'

Now she really couldn't make sense of things at all. 'Wh-what?' was all that came out.

Her joints ached. She looked down. These weren't her PJs. She wrinkled her nose as she realised she was wearing a hospital gown. She pulled it away from her body. 'What?' she asked again.

'You haven't been well,' Duc said quickly, his face grave. 'You have malaria. We think you got bitten while helping at the accident—you had short sleeves that day.'

Malaria? 'But I take the meds...'

His hand was still touching hers. It was almost like he didn't want to let go.

'I know,' he said, then shook his head. 'But for some reason they've not worked. They're doing some special bloodwork to find out more.'

He looked at her seriously. 'Why didn't you tell me you weren't feeling well? The night sweats? The head-aches? Was there anything else?'

She honestly couldn't remember right now. Plus, right now this felt like a bit of a lecture.

'I need to sleep,' she said firmly, closing her eyes and curling on her side again. Next time she woke up she'd complain about these sheets and the hospital gown...

It was four days before Viv was anything like normal again. She was cranky, and constantly tired. It had to be expected. She still couldn't seem to get her head around the fact she'd contracted malaria.

All the hospital staff kept popping in. Joe was a con-stant, as was Duc, with an occasional visit from Lien, who was still suffering from her hyperemesis gravi-darum. Ron had even dropped in on a few occasions, bringing tea and sitting down to chat.

She still couldn't believe this had happened to her. Now, in hindsight, she remembered having an itch on the back of her arm. But she'd never even thought to look at it in the mirror. She'd been too busy. There had been too much else going on.

Too much Duc...

Today she'd managed to persuade him to let her go back and sleep in her own bed. At least, that was how she still thought of it. But he'd insisted on carrying her the whole way.

She hadn't been amused.

She'd also had to promise that people could come in and 'check' on her. It seemed no one was listening when she insisted she was a nurse and could look after herself.

The bungalow was a lot tidier since the last time she'd

been here. 'What happened to all the boxes?' she asked as Duc carried her through the main room.

He had the good grace to look sheepish. 'Mai Ahn. When you collapsed, I took you straight across to the hospital and stayed with you. I kind of forgot we'd been in the middle of things. But Mai Ahn came and asked if she could do anything to help and offered to take the boxes to goodwill for me.'

Of course. They'd been in the middle of emptying out his parents' things. She remembered the emotions on his face. How final it all must have seemed to him.

'Sorry,' she muttered.

'What?' he looked surprised. 'What have you got to be sorry for?'

She waved her hand. She couldn't look at him right now. It seemed that now she'd woken up, all the emotions she'd kept locked away these past few months were fighting to get out now. It seemed that being sick had used up all the firm reserves she normally had.

If she looked at Duc, with his floppy hair and soft brown eyes, she would crumble.

'I think I need to leave,' were the words that came out. 'As soon as I feel better. I think I need to leave.'

'What?' His voice was incredulous.

She concentrated on her hands. 'This isn't working out—not for me, Duc.'

'But I thought you liked it here?'

'I do. I mean I did.'

Her hands had never looked so interesting.

'Viv, talk to me. Tell me what you mean?'

How could she do that? How could she tell her best friend that their relationship could never be the same again—at least, not for her?

From the instant she'd stepped off the plane and seen him again, things had changed between them.

It was nobody's fault.

Neither of them understood the change, but they'd crossed a line for Viv. No matter how hard she tried, she couldn't ignore the spark of attraction she felt for Duc now.

She'd never felt so connected to a person, or a place.

'I can't st-stay. Not here. Not now.'

He thumped down on the bed next to her. She closed her eyes. She could smell him. The familiar scents she associated with Duc. The laundry detergent he used for his clothes. How many times had she cuddled him, or lain with her head against his shoulder breathing that in?

He swung his legs up on to the bed so he was sitting parallel with her. She could almost hear his brain spinning, trying to find words. She knew him. Sometimes she thought she knew him better than he knew himself.

She took a deep breath. 'You've done well, Duc. This place is great. You've sorted things out. You can go back now. You can go back and be the surgeon you've always wanted to be.'

There was a long pause. 'You think that's what I want to do?'

'I know that's what you want to do. You should live the life you want.' Her voice started to shake a little. 'You should be happy.'

'What if I told you that's not what makes me happy?'

She jerked, and automatically turned to face him, cursing herself for letting down her guard.

His brown eyes were fixed straight on her. Sincere.

'Viv, what if I told you that it might have taken me a

number of years to figure out, but the thing that makes me happy is you.'

She felt herself start to shake. She shook her head. 'No. No, it's not, Duc.'

His voice was steady. He reached over and intertwined his pinkie with hers. She wanted to pull her hand away, but the warmth from his skin seemed to hold her there.

'Viv, I'm sorry. I never really tried to walk in your shoes. I never really understood what your life must be like. You always seemed so independent, so self-sufficient, as if it was what you wanted, what you needed. I just didn't think any further than that. I didn't look deep enough when I should have.'

She didn't know quite where this conversation was going. 'What do you mean?'

He ran his other hand through his hair. 'I thought we told each other everything. I thought we were best friends. But when I look back, I've not been the friend that I should have.' This time it was his gaze that dropped to their intertwined pinkies. 'I let you down. I should have realised—I should have understood.'

She could feel herself starting to panic—she couldn't quite follow where he was going with this. 'What do you mean?'

'All those bad boyfriends. All the no-hopers and ratbags. The one guy you went out with who was actually nice—Archie? Remember him?'

She felt herself shudder. She still couldn't understand what this conversation was about. Archie. Yes, of course she remembered him. The electrician from Bristol. A lovely guy, good-natured, hard-working and hopelessly devoted with a good sense of humour. She'd dumped him after a few months. Archie had been nice. Archie had been safe. Archie would have looked after her. There wasn't a single bad thing she could say about him.

She nodded without speaking.

'You ran, Viv. You ran so fast you practically sprinted. Because Archie could have offered you an attachment. Love.' He bit his bottom lip. 'A home. But you couldn't do it. You couldn't cope. And everyone you picked after that? They could offer none of those things. I didn't see it at the time. I didn't understand. But you deliberately went for guys like that because they would never make you form an attachment. You didn't need to invest your heart in them. It was like you predetermined every relationship. And I think you did it without even realising why.'

Her skin prickled as he spoke. There was something so achingly familiar about some of the things he was saying. She actually felt nauseous. She wanted to be indignant. She wanted to automatically shout and deny every part of this. But too much of it was making her feel uncomfortable. Too much of it sounded so close to the truth that it made her stomach hurt.

And it seemed that Duc didn't know when to stop. 'You run, Viv. You run because it's easier than stopping to find out if love and home are actually worth the heartache.'

Now she snapped and snatched her hand away from his. 'Not all of us had the life you did, Duc. Not all of us had Khiem and Hoa.' It was cruel to bring them up when only a few months before they'd been snatched away from their son, but it seemed like now it was time for no holds barred.

'But when do you stop running, Viv? When do you

stop and catch your breath? When do you take the time to look around and decide if someone and somewhere might actually be worth the risk?'

She could almost hear his heart in those words. There was a pleading tone to his voice.

'I could have lost you. I invited you here. You contracted a disease that's endemic to my country. I invited you to a place that could have killed you. I've spent the last few days scared to breathe, Viv. Scared that every breath might be the last one with you by my side. I had no idea. No idea what I had. And every idea about what I might lose.'

Her heart gave a little flip. Where was this going? She wanted to speak. She wanted to say something. But all the words were just gummed up in her mouth.

'You taught me about here. You let me learn to love being a doctor again. Not a surgeon, a *doctor*. You made me realise just what I've got here. Not just a building, but the people too. I can't imagine leaving. I can't imagine ever working anywhere else.' He took a deep breath. 'But I will. If you want me to.'

She frowned. 'What?'

He took a few moments. 'I want you to be happy, Viv. And if staying here isn't something you can contemplate, then tell me where you want to go, and I'll come too.'

She shook her head. 'What are you talking about?'

He pointed to his chest. 'Me.' Then pointed at hers. 'You. We have to give this a chance. We have to give us a chance. We have to see if this, us, is meant to be.' He reached over and gently touched her cheek. 'Let me show you what home can be.'

Maybe it was the way he said the words. Or maybe it

was some of the stuff he'd said before, but every hackle went up at the back of her neck.

Her stomach plummeted. This was so not what she wanted to hear. He felt sorry for her. It was like he was still in doctor mode. 'You can't fix me, Duc.' She shook her head and tried to stop the tears forming in her eyes. 'Even if all the stuff you think about me is true, I'm scared to form relationships, I'm scared to take a chance on a home. I'm not your charity project. You don't get to feel sorry for me. And what you never get to do is...' she lifted her fingers in the air '...fix me.'

The very thought repulsed her. This wasn't what she wanted. In every tiny splintered dream she'd imagined what they could become to each other, and this wasn't it.

Duc gave a bewildered smile and shook his head. 'I don't want to fix you, Viv. That's not why I'm here. You don't need fixing. You're perfect just the way you are.'

'So what are you trying to say?'

He fixed his deep brown eyes on hers. 'What I'm asking for is permission to love you.'

She froze. Was that really just what he'd said?

'But...but you pulled away. You didn't want us to go down that path. You pulled away as if it was the worst thing you'd ever thought of. As if kissing me was the worst thing you'd ever done. Then you made an excuse about us just staying friends.'

He let out a wry laugh. 'Really? You thought I didn't like kissing you?' He looked incredulous. 'Viv, when you're wrong, you're *so* wrong it's scary.'

She scowled as he used one of her own expressions, mimicking her Scottish accent.

'Viv, I've thought about kissing you from practically the moment you stepped off that plane in those denim shorts and that tied-up shirt. From the second you wrapped your arms around me at the airport something changed. At least, for me it did. Every casual hug or brush of your hand just seems to set me crazy—in a good way. I spend my life sniffing for that orange-blossom scent from your shampoo, wondering where you are. You sent my blood pressure skyrocketing in your "interview" outfit. As for that red dress?' He shook his head again, his smile reaching his twinkling eyes.

'I have no idea why we didn't go down this road before. Maybe we just both weren't ready. Maybe we weren't at that point in our lives. Maybe we needed to both find our feet a little. But now? Now, Viv? I'm ready if you are. Just say the word. Because I want to love you, Viv. I do. I want us to try and be together. More than anything in this world. More than this place. More than the other hospitals. I want to try with me and you. So, just say the word. Say that you'll give us a chance. It can be anywhere in the world. I'll follow you anywhere you want to go, Viv. Just tell me that you think we're worth a chance.'

She was stunned. This conversation had started in a very different way. She wasn't quite sure how after all this time Duc had just managed to say a million things at once.

'You have no idea—' his voice was lower, more gravelly '—what it felt like to see you collapse. To see you lying in that hospital bed. I lost my mum and dad this year, Viv. The thought of losing you too? I couldn't handle that. I can't handle losing the person I need most. I'm not crazy. I know I'm not crazy. But things have changed between us. We both know that. So let's take this, let's grab it with both hands and see where it takes us. We've got to be worth a try, surely, Viv.' He lowered his voice even more. 'I know I want to, with all my heart.'

A single tear slid down her cheek. She looked over at him. Now she saw it. Now she saw the fact he hadn't slept properly in days. The lines around his eyes.

She took a deep breath. 'It's not your fault I got sick. That's life. I was taking precautions, but I did go out to the accident in short sleeves. I didn't think about it—and I didn't notice any mosquito bite. That's my fault, not yours. But—' she locked gazes with him '—you haven't really told me how you feel about me, Duc. You say you want to try—but why do you want to try?'

He looked confused for a moment.

She held out her hands. 'This place is…different too. For me, that is. Maybe it is an age and stage thing, but I finally feel as if I've found a place I can fit in. I can be me. I like the people. I like the patients. The only thing that stops me wanting to stay here is you.'

He looked shocked. 'Why?'

She shook her head. 'You can't stay because it seems like a good idea. You can't stay because you think I want to. You dreamed of being a surgeon. Is that dream still there? Because if it is, in a few months you'll start to be miserable and unhappy. You won't want to be here, and it will affect everyone around you.'

He shook his head. He looked out the window across to the hospital. 'I'd never taken the time I've had here to look at things. You know what surgical teams are like? It's a back-stabbing competitive world. I thought that was how I wanted to live my life. But after a while I realised just how much more of a doctor I can be here. I'm still adjusting. But there's so much work to be done that I don't want to stand still. I want to keep this place moving and make sure we're doing all we can. This is a job of a lifetime, Viv—at least, for me. I know you've moved about. I know you might still want to. You asked me how I really feel about you? I love you. I think I might always have loved you. If this place doesn't make you happy...' he put his hand to his chest '...and I don't make you happy, then I want you to know that I will always love you, I will always be here, I will always be your best friend. And...' he slowed down '...you will always have a home here, with me.'

She started to sob. She couldn't help it, and Duc moved, wrapping one arm around her shoulders and pulling her close.

'I love this place,' she said between sniffs as she laid her hand on his chest. 'But I love this place because it's got you in it. It is you. Everywhere I look I'm reminded of you. I couldn't be here if you weren't. You drive me crazy, do you know that? You kissed me in the kitchen and then pulled away. Do you know what that did to me? What that did to my heart? I thought it might break in two.'

He kissed her head. 'I'm sorry, Viv. I was mixed up. I thought I'd crossed a line and ruined everything between us. I thought you'd hate me.'

Her hand thumped against his chest. 'How can I hate you when I love you, stupid? The guy who's been my everything for the last ten years. The one person I'm honest with and tell all my dark family secrets.' She fingered the chain at her throat.

'The one man to buy me jewellery just because it matched my eyes. And when you kissed me...you turned my world upside down. A kiss between friends isn't supposed to feel like *that*. Isn't supposed to steal the breath from your throat and turn your legs to jelly. Isn't supposed to leave your heart racing so much you can't sleep at night.' Her fingers were brushing the skin at the base of his neck. He looked down at her with those dark eyes. She could see the sparkle. Feel the sizzle in the air between them again.

She moved her fingers more slowly. 'And this? This electricity that constantly buzzes between us? How are we ever supposed to get any work done in future? How will any patients ever get seen if we both work here?'

She couldn't help the teasing tone in her voice. Her heart was so full she couldn't breathe again. Duc loved her. He said he loved her. Could the world ever be this perfect?

He changed position, tilting her chin up to his. 'So, this is us. This is really us.'

It was like he was just making sure.

She nodded.

But he kept going as a sexy smile appeared on his face. 'No pulling back. No changing minds?'

'No pulling back, no changing minds,' she repeated with a smile on her face, then she sighed as he jumped off the bed and headed to the doorway. 'Duc, are you ever going to kiss me? Or am I going to have to die waiting?'

'Oh, I'm going to kiss you, I'm just making sure we'll not be disturbed.' He smiled as he turned the lock on the door and joined her back on the bed. He slid his arms around her waist. 'Now, where were we?'

'Right here,' she said as her lips touched his.

CHAPTER FIFTEEN

Six months later

'PUSH, LIEN. PUSH!'

It was the middle of the night. But no one at May Mắn hospital currently cared what time of day it was.

The corridor outside the delivery room was practically full. This was their first official May Mắn baby, created by two doctors who worked there, delivered by staff who loved them both.

Duc was pacing outside. Lien's parents were sitting impatiently on two chairs, watching for every swing of the door. Several of the nurses had lined the corridor. Two of the visiting doctors who were officially on duty tonight were watching the whole scene with amusement.

They'd even started to serve snacks while they waited.

Every now and then Viv stuck her head outside with an instruction for someone and they all held their breaths, letting them go in frustration when she still didn't bring the news they were all waiting for.

Ron was the most amused of all. There was a coloured chart at the nurses' station with guesses for date, time, sex, birth weight and name. 'Is it always going to be this much fun?' he said as he walked past.

For a few minutes there was silence. Then came a loud cry.

A cheer erupted from outside as Baby Lennox announced her arrival to the world. Viv cleaned off her face, did a few quick checks and placed baby on Lien's chest.

Lien wrinkled her nose as she lay back against the pillows, exhausted. 'Tell me they aren't high-fiving out there.'

Viv and Ron laughed together. 'It's been a closely fought contest. Three staff were watching the clock, hoping they'd win the bet.'

Lien shook her head as she stared at her brand-new daughter. 'Wow,' she breathed. Then she looked at Joe. He hadn't taken his eyes off his daughter from the second she'd been born. 'I'm not doing that again.'

Viv and Ron looked at each other. 'That's what they all say,' they said in unison.

Lien smiled. 'I mean it.'

Viv nodded. 'So do they. It doesn't mean that in two years' time I won't see you again.'

Ron grinned. 'Well, I'm delighted. Do we have a name for our latest arrival?'

Joe sighed. 'Nope. We both agreed we would give Regan the final say, and since we didn't know if it was a boy or a girl, he said he was keeping his name a secret.'

Ron let out the biggest laugh of all. 'Yes! I can't wait.' He stood up. 'We were talking about his favourite superhero the other day so hold on, folks, who knows what we'll get?'

Five minutes later Lien and the baby were settled, and Viv had cleaned up the room for visitors, meaning the rest of the hospital could visit.

Duc shook hands with Joe and gave Lien a kiss on the cheek after admiring the baby, and waved to Viv to come outside.

Viv left things in the hands of Melody, the other midwife, and walked outside with him to sit on the grass for five minutes.

It was cooler outside, and once he'd wrapped an arm around her shoulder she leaned against him.

'Ooh, I'm knackered. You need to make me some tea.'

His breathing was slow and steady. She could actually stay in this position all night. They sometimes sat outside for a short spell at night, just to watch the stars.

It took her a few moments to notice something unusual. 'Hey? What's happened to the trees?'

'What do you mean?'

She sat upright. 'What's with the twinkling lights?'

Someone had strung little white lights between the trees to the left of the bungalows. They'd put a memorial bench under the trees a few months ago for Khiem and Hoa.

'Oh, *those* lights,' said Duc, as he stood up and held his hand out towards her.

She smiled but wrinkled her brow in curiosity as he led her towards the bench. They watched as Joe crossed the grass behind them, ducking into his own bungalow to collect Regan and let him meet his new sister.

Viv sat down on the bench and looked up at the lights. 'They really do add a little magic to the place, don't they? We should have thought of these before. And maybe, at Christmastime, we can change them for another colour?'

She looked to her right, expecting Duc to be beside her, but he'd vanished.

'Duc?'

'Right here.'

He was kneeling on the grass in front of her.

She let out a little gasp and pulled both hands up to her mouth.

He smiled. 'Timing is everything.'

He took her hands in his. 'Viv, the last six months have been the best of my life. You're my partner in crime and the love of my life. I can't imagine spending a minute of this life without having you by my side. I can't imagine a day when you don't shout at me in your crazy Scottish accent or fight me for a bit of chocolate. Let's not wait. It's been too long already.'

He pulled out the glittering emerald-and-diamond ring that had belonged to his mother. 'You know that my mum and dad loved you.' He glanced upwards. 'Somehow I know that right now they're up there, smiling down on us and telling me to hurry up.' He shot her a wary look. 'If you want something else, I'll buy you something else. But my mum always told me she hoped I'd find someone to love, like she loved Dad. And maybe she already knew who that would be. So, what do you say, Vivienne Kerr, crazy Scot number one, will you be my wife, for ever and ever?'

Her hands were shaking, but that didn't stop her holding out her finger so he could slip the emerald-and-diamond ring onto it. She touched his cheek. 'Duc Nguyen, I got so lucky the day I met you. I can't imagine what might have happened if you hadn't been there to give me a hug in the sluice that day. You've stolen my heart, and you've given me something I couldn't ever have found without you—a home. And the ring? I love it. I'm honoured. So, yes! Tell the world that, yes, I'll be your wife.'

Duc swept her up into his arms and spun her around but when her feet touched the ground she took a step back for a second until she found his hand.

She linked their pinkies together and looked up into his eyes. 'For ever,' she whispered.

'For ever,' he repeated as he bent to kiss her.

* * * * *

LET'S TALK
Romance

For exclusive extracts, competitions
and special offers, find us online:

f facebook.com/millsandboon

◉ @millsandboonuk

▼ @millsandboon

Or get in touch on 0844 844 1351*

For all the latest titles coming soon,
visit millsandboon.co.uk/nextmonth

*Calls cost 7p per minute plus your phone company's price per
minute access charge

Want even more
ROMANCE?

Join our bookclub today!

'Mills & Boon books, the perfect way to escape for an hour or so.'

Miss W. Dyer

'Excellent service, promptly delivered and very good subscription choices.'

Miss A. Pearson

'You get fantastic special offers and the chance to get books before they hit the shops'

Mrs V. Hall

Visit millsandbook.co.uk/Bookclub and save on brand new books.

MILLS & BOON